5 TIMES REVENGE

LINDSAY ELAND

GREENWILLOW BOOKS
An Imprint of HarperCollinsPublishers

Five Times Revenge
Copyright © 2016 by Lindsay Eland

The text of this book is set in 12-point Janson Text.
Book design by Paul Zakris

Library of Congress Cataloging-in-Publication Data is available.
ISBN 978-0-06-239730-0 (trade ed.)
16 17 18 19 20 PC/RRDH 10 9 8 7 6 5 4 3 2 1
First Edition

 Greenwillow Books

For Rebecca and Martha, co-conspirators.
And for Gracie, Isaac, Ella, Noah, and John-boy . . . always.

CHAPTER 1

Adam

Not many eighth graders arrive early to their middle school in the morning, at least not on purpose. They usually spill out of squeaky bus doors, or dash down the sidewalk with only minutes to spare, hoping to avoid the secretary and her tapping foot and waiting red pen. They slip into chairs just as the bell rings or hand over the late notice. They're never early.

But there was only one April 1st out of the whole year, and there was only one Adam Baker.

Sort of like there is only one Harry Potter, one Percy Jackson, one Cinderella.

Of course, Adam Baker wasn't a wizard or a demigod and definitely not a princess.

He was just a normal, ordinary eighth grader . . . but then again, who or what is ordinary?

After locking his bike to the metal rack, Adam scanned the parking lot and waited for his best friend, Perk, to arrive. The secretary, Mrs. Gingko, and the janitor, Mr. Jelepy, were usually the only people who arrived this early. Sure enough, there was Mrs. Gingko's small Ford Escort parked in the employee parking lot, and Mr. Jelepy's bike was locked next to Adam's. But there was no sign of Principal Parmar's pristine Shelby Cobra.

Mr. Parmar, the principal of Anderson Middle School, and his high-and-mighty son, Hill, hated Adam's guts and everything surrounding his guts and on top of his guts and then all the blood and bones and skin in between his guts.

The feeling was mutual.

Perk said Principal Parmar hated Adam because he knew that Adam was smarter than he was. Mr. Parmar loved to brag about how he got a perfect score on his SATs and his ACTs and all the other three-letter tests out there that a man needs to take in order to become a principal of a middle-sized middle school.

Adam knew he wasn't smarter than Mr. Parmar—not in a test score way—but he *did* know all of Mr. Parmar's computer passwords. He knew that Mr. Parmar had a prescription for chronic foot fungus, and that he had been caught cheating on his teachers exam in college and had to retake it . . . twice.

Adam was smarter in a more useful way.

And Perk said that Principal Parmar's son, Hill, hated Adam's guts because Adam beat him in everything—whether it was the fifty-yard dash, or a race to finish a cupcake first. It actually had become a sort of game for Adam. Really, Adam knew going into each "competition" that he could lose. Hill was more athletic, he was stronger, he had a bigger appetite, and he was more handsome. But when Adam acted like he *didn't* care if he won or lost, it unhinged Hill.

Adam didn't think either of those things was the reason Mr. Parmar and Hill hated his guts.

It was because Adam couldn't—he *wouldn't*—be pushed around.

He laughed when Hill taped a "kick me" sign to his back (was Hill really that uncreative?) or threw him against a locker or dumped milk on his lunch (it was disgusting, true, but better to eat a sandwich swimming in chocolate milk than give Hill any satisfaction). And when he found his absences had mysteriously gone from a few days to a few weeks, he made sure that it was on the record that he hadn't missed a day in three years.

"Hey."

Adam looked up and grinned at his best friend. "You ready?"

"Let's do it," Perk said. He took a bite of the chocolate-frosted donut in his hand and held out the bag to Adam. "Glazed? Last one."

Glazed were his favorite. Actually, any sort of donut was his favorite. If it was fried and then dusted with sugar or cinnamon or sugar *and* cinnamon or covered in frosting, it was his favorite. Adam reached in the bag and pulled it out. "Thanks. You have the tape and the Vaseline?"

Perk tossed him a roll of Scotch tape and a small jar. "You have the signs?"

Adam stuck the donut in his mouth without biting into it and unzipped his backpack, pulling out a stack of white papers. He handed Perk half of them before taking a proper bite of his donut. He said through chews, "I'll go this way and you go that way. We'll meet at the back doors and then go inside."

Perk nodded. "See ya in a few."

Adam ate his donut and made his way around all the outside doors, taping "WET PAINT. PLEASE USE OTHER DOOR" signs on the panes of glass. The thought of the endless circle of students and teachers walking from door to door around the building brought a smile to his face.

He and Perk met at the back of the school. "You want to do the honors?" Adam asked.

Perk punched in the teachers' code for the doors and they walked in.

"I'll take everything from the cafeteria to the Spanish and French rooms," Perk said, starting off down the hall to the stairs.

Adam nodded. "I'll do the rest. Meet you at Parmar's office in fifteen."

Within twenty minutes they had hung up all the signs on the doors. Adam chuckled when the first bell rang and the halls were still relatively empty— everyone still circling outside trying to figure out where to come in.

Mrs. Gingko sat in her red swivel chair inside the main office eating an orange, one painful slice at a time—the juice splurting out in more directions than Adam could have thought. Principal Parmar's office was just behind her, the doorknob practically begging to be slathered in the slippery Vaseline.

Adam looked at Perk and smiled. "Ready for the door?"

"I'll distract her." Perk walked up to Mrs. Gingko and Mrs. Gingko's orange—which dotted the front of Perk's coat with a stream of juice. "Hi, Mrs. Gingko," he said.

She looked up. "What do you need, dear?"

Perk shrugged. "Oh, Mr. Parmar asked me to come and get you to help take down those signs on all the doors. A dumb prank, it looks like."

Mrs. Gingko stood up, leaving the rest of the orange seeping through a piece of paper towel. She sighed. "Where is he?"

"He said he was taking the ones down on this side of the school and asked if you could take down the rest on the other side of the school."

Perk and Adam watched her click-clack down the hallway.

Then they walked into the main office, straight for Principal Parmar's closed office door. Adam pulled out the Vaseline and slathered the doorknob with a thick layer. He stepped back and nodded his head.

Perk smiled. "That'll keep him busy for a while."

Just then, Parmar's voice echoed from just down the hall and his walkie-talkie blared. "What are you doing at the other end of the school, Debbie?" he said. "Get down here."

"He's coming," Adam whispered. He tucked the Vaseline in his pocket.

Static followed and Mrs. Gingko "ten-four-ed" back.

Adam and Perk ducked into the nurse's office as Parmar walked in. Mrs. Zelinsky, the music teacher, followed after him, wiping her hands on a paper towel.

"You've got to do something. He's becoming a menace in the hallways. Stuffing kids in lockers, flushing homework, not to mention that just last week he hung William Bubert in the teachers' lounge by his underwear." She cringed. "The poor boy couldn't walk for days. And just now I caught him supergluing Dutch Walker's locker shut, so not only is Mr. Jelepy going to have to get the locker open, but Dutch is going to have to get another lock. You know that he and his grandfather are barely making it."

Mr. Parmar looked down at Mrs. Gingko's orange and popped a slice into his mouth. "Now, Paula," he said, and Adam watched him touch her lightly on the shoulder. "I think that's quite an exaggeration. They're all kids. Hill is just doing what they all do. Unfortunately, because he's my son—the principal's son—he seems to get more attention from teachers."

Mrs. Zelinsky shrugged off his hand. "You know that isn't true. He gets into trouble with us because he gets himself into trouble."

Mr. Parmar picked up Mrs. Gingko's calendar and flipped through it. "I don't know about that, Paula. But . . ." He paused. "Teacher reviews are coming up next week. And you're scheduled for Tuesday, I think."

"Yes."

"Well, you can bring it up then if you'd like."

"Yes, I think I will."

"How's your husband, Rick, doing? Any luck with finding a job?"

"No, not yet. But he has—"

"I'm sure he's glad that you still have a good position," Mr. Parmar interrupted.

Mrs. Zelinsky looked as if she was about to respond, then stopped. They were both quiet, and Adam watched as they stared at each other like two cowboys facing off in a swirl of dust.

Mr. Parmar spoke first. "Now, I know we both have things to do. I'll see you next Tuesday at your review, and we can discuss the issue with Hill then."

"No," Mrs. Zelinsky said. "It's all right. I don't need to bring it up again."

Mr. Parmar nodded. "If you're sure." He turned to his office and was about to place a hand on the slippery doorknob when he looked back. "And you'd better get to your classroom, Paula. The second bell will ring any moment, and we need to start the day on time."

Adam watched her turn on her heel and click down the hall. He turned to Perk, who shook his head in disgust.

"What do you say we reset the clock?" Adam whispered.

"And I'll turn up the volume on the loudspeaker."

"Perfect."

Mr. Parmar twisted and turned the doorknob to his office. "Dang it. What is this? Debbie! Where is that woman?"

Using his shirt to twist the knob, he finally pulled it open. Adam wished Parmar would turn around so that he could see the greasy smear, but Mr. Parmar stepped inside and slammed the door.

Adam and Perk slipped from their hiding place.

"Penny him in," Adam said, tossing Perk a dull penny. "We'll give him some extra time to think about the upcoming teacher reviews. Mrs. Gingko will be back any minute. I'll take care of the loudspeaker."

Perk grinned and jammed the penny in the crease of the office door. He then adjusted the clock while Adam turned the volume up on the announcement speaker to its highest point.

Later on, at lunch, Adam and Perk overheard Scott say that it took two hours for Mr. Jelepy to get Parmar out of his office.

It pays to be early for school sometimes.

CHAPTER 2
Perk

His full name was Perkins Benjamin Irving.

But that was only on his birth certificate.

And only his mom and dad, Adam's parents, and teachers on the first day of school ever called him Perkins. To his grandparents he was "Gingi" on account of his red hair. All other times he was Perk.

Simple. Short. To the point. That's how Perk liked things, for the most part. But his older brother, Tommy, was definitely not simple or short or to the point.

But that was Tommy, the exception.

Exception: a person or thing that is excluded from a general statement or does not follow a rule.

Perk lived mostly in the background—watching, looking, taking things in, listening. And in all his watching, looking, taking things in, and listening, Perk had found that pretty much everything and everyone has an exception to their rules. Perk knew he had some exceptions, but generally he didn't think he had many.

The final bell rang. Perk stopped at his locker and pulled out his backpack.

Adam knocked him on the shoulder. "Hey, I'm headed to the restaurant. Is this the day Tommy has his art class after school?"

"Yep. Every. Single. Monday and Wednesday."

"I'll tag along with you to the high school and then keep going."

"Cool."

Once outside, Perk and Adam threaded through the clusters of kids getting on buses or in a parent's car and started toward the high school. He'd taken the bag of sour gummies out of his pocket because the warm spring sun was making them mush together and Tommy didn't like them mushy or warm.

"Tommy's favorite?" Adam asked, kicking a rock along the sidewalk.

Perk watched the rock skip ahead of them and then took a turn sending it careening down the cement. "Yep."

They continued like this, taking turns swiping at the rock, until they arrived at the school. A line of students was already standing in the overgrown grass with the teachers, waiting for their parents to come by and pick them up. Perk spotted Nish getting into her mother's red car. Tommy had had a crush on her the entire school year.

Perk turned his gaze back to the line, expecting to see Tommy craning his neck to find him like he always did on Monday afternoon, but he wasn't there.

"Well, look who's here," Adam said, pointing to Mr. Parmar's Shelby Cobra. "Our dear old principal."

Perk sneered. "Yuck. Wonder what he's here for?"

Mrs. Pell, one of Tommy's teachers, smiled when Perk walked up. "Hi, Perk. Adam," she said. "Tommy went into the bathroom real quick. He should be out in a minute, but you're welcome to go inside. Just remember to check out with me before you leave."

"Thanks."

The two of them walked into the school through

the classroom entrance with Perk leading the way to the hallway bathroom.

"You're right," Adam said, glancing around. "This place has gotten worse since the last time I was here."

"I know." Perk pushed open the boys' bathroom. "Hey, Tommy? It's Perk. Adam's here, too."

Nothing.

Perk looked back at Adam, but he was picking at the peeling paint on the walls.

"Tommy?"

Silence.

He stepped in and checked under the stalls. Weird.

"Did we miss him somehow?"

"We couldn't have," Perk said. He let the door close behind him. "We would have passed each other in the hall."

He sighed. Short. To the point. Concise. Planned out. Routine. That was how Perk kept everything. That was how he liked it. Tommy went to the bathroom and added a glitch to the system. Perk would just fix it.

He headed back down the hallway to Tommy's classroom. Propping open the door was a red brick, and though the room was dark, Perk stuck his head inside. "Tommy?"

Again, nothing.

"Tommy?" Adam echoed. "Do you think he's hiding from us?"

Perk shook his head and peered down the hallway. "No way. This is his favorite part of the day. He only hides when he has to get a haircut or my mom makes homemade pizza which, thankfully, isn't that often."

"Where should we look?"

There was the sound of high heels, and Mrs. Pell came around the corner and walked toward them. "Hi, boys," she said. "Sorry, I got tied up with Principal Parmar and his son. They just left." She sighed and looked around. "Where's Tommy?"

"He wasn't in the bathroom and he isn't in here," Perk said. He felt his breath shorten. "We were going to check the other rooms."

"What? Where could he have gone? That isn't like him." Mrs. Pell turned on her heel. "I'll check down by the office. Adam, check by the picnic tables—just go out the side door of my classroom. And Perk, you go down by the gym."

Seeing Mrs. Pell's panic flipped Perk's heart inside his chest, up and over and around. If his skin were see-through plastic, his stomach and heart and liver would look like a washing machine, everything churning and spinning.

"He could be anywhere." Perk glanced up and down the hallway again as if Tommy would be strolling toward them. The churning inside him threatened to bring his lunch up.

"Hey," Adam said, grabbing onto his shirt. Perk looked at him. "We'll find him."

"Yeah, okay."

They'd find him. They had to. He couldn't have gone far. They'd look everywhere and then they'd find him.

Every passing minute felt like an hour. Perk checked the gym, the other bathrooms, and the art and music room and was about to call his parents and the police when he heard a noise coming from behind a door labeled "Utility Room."

He put his ear up against it. "Tommy?"

The crying grew louder and Perk pulled on the doorknob.

Locked.

"Tommy, it's me, Perk. It's okay. Just give me a second while I go find the key." He dashed down the hallway and yelled for Mrs. Pell, who came running, along with two other teachers Perk didn't know. "He's locked in the maintenance room."

A minute later, the door opened and Tommy fell into Perk's arms crying, snot and spit streaking his face, his round cheeks flushed a deep red. His pants were wet, and a sign was taped to his back that said, "Kick me, I'm retarded."

"Sorry, Perk," he sobbed. "I'm sorry. I don't know where my friends went. I'm sorry. Don't be mad. Don't be mad. I'm sorry."

"What happened, Tommy?" Mrs. Pell said. She put one hand on his shoulder and the other on Perk's.

"It's okay, Tommy," Perk heard himself say. He ripped the paper from his brother's backpack and crumpled it in his fist, tighter and tighter until he felt his nails digging into his skin. Perk hadn't cried since the fourth grade, but now his eyes stung with relief mixed with boiling anger. Who were these so-called friends?

Adam was suddenly there, and Tommy released

Perk and hugged Adam. "Oh man, Tommy, are we ever glad to see you. What happened?"

Tommy swiped his arm across his nose. He let go of Adam and then hugged Mrs. Pell and the other teachers in turn. "My friends said that we could play hide-and-seek together. One told me to hide in here. I did, but then I couldn't get out and . . ."

While Tommy continued, Perk passed the sign to Adam, his pulse pattering in his chest, anger rushing through his veins so hard and thick and powerful that he wished there was something nearby that he could punch.

Or some*one*.

Adam read the note quickly, his face whitening. Mrs. Pell must've been looking over Adam's shoulder because she grabbed the paper from his hand. "What is this?" she said, her voice growing shrill as she read it again. "Who wrote this?" She passed it to one of the other teachers. "Oh, Tommy . . ."

Then, as quickly as the expression crossed Adam's face it was gone, and he threw his arm around Tommy. "Come on. Why don't we all go to the restaurant and have some ice cream?"

Tommy sniffled again. "Really? Can we, Perk? Adam's restaurant is my favorite. I think we should. I love ice cream. With lots of whipped cream, because I love whipped cream. It's my very, very favorite."

"Yeah, sure. Can I take my brother home now, Mrs. Pell?"

"Your parents need to know what happened," she said. "Tommy has a spare set of clothes in his cubby. He can change into those while I call them."

Perk nodded and picked up Tommy's backpack, then he and Adam walked down the hall to the bathroom, Tommy in between them.

While Tommy changed, Adam looked over at Perk. "Don't worry," he said quietly. "We'll find out who it was. We'll make them pay."

Perk nodded and swiped at his eyes.

They walked to Bakers' Place—the restaurant that Adam's parents owned and operated—and sat down in Tommy's favorite spot, the booth by the second window, so that he could look out at the birds that lived in the oak tree out front.

Adam stood and headed toward the kitchen. "I

have to check in with my parents. I'll be back. Three sundaes?"

Tommy smiled. "With lots of whipped cream!"

"Please," Perk prompted.

"Please," Tommy mimicked.

A few minutes later, Adam walked over with a tray and set down three ice cream sundaes, one with a tower of whipped cream and a thick line of it edged around the bowl. "Here you go," he said, taking a seat.

Just then, a spitball hit Adam on the ear. Hill Parmar sat with a pack of his friends and his dad at a table a little ways off. "Hey, Baker, how about some service over here?" Hill called. Principal Parmar chuckled and shook his head.

But Perk didn't feel bad for Adam.

You didn't feel bad for Adam. Ever. If anyone should feel bad for someone it was Hill, because Adam would take care of him.

Eventually.

Tommy looked up from his ice cream. He waved at Hill and his friend. "Hey! Hi! Remember me? Tommy. I'm Tommy."

Hill looked over at Tommy and, though it was

subtle, Perk watched Hill's eyes widen for a moment and then shift away. Perk knew. Perk met Adam's eyes. Adam knew, too.

Tommy knocked Perk with his elbow. "Those are my friends, Perk. My new friends."

He continued on, even though Perk knew the rest of the story. "Where did you guys go? You're good hiders. I got locked in a room but my brother found me. I can't ever do something like that again. Ever. Right, Perk?"

Hill shrugged. "I don't know what you're talking about."

"That's my son"—Mr. Parmar smiled—"making friends wherever he goes."

Perk started to stand, but Adam grabbed his arm. "Not yet."

Perk nodded, unclenching his fist. He was right.

As they stood up to leave a little while later, Perk held out the piece of paper so that Hill and Mr. Parmar could read the blue permanent marker. "I bet the handwriting will be pretty easy to match. And lucky for me, my parents are lawyers."

Mr. Parmar grabbed Perk's arm and smiled so wide

that Perk noticed how gray his teeth were. "I'm sure this is just a big mistake, Perkins, right?" He reached for the piece of paper.

Perk jerked his arm away and tucked the paper into his back pocket.

He smiled back.

He didn't like taking revenge, usually.

But everyone has their exceptions.

CHAPTER 3
Adam

Adam sat down with his brown-paper-bag lunch and waited for Perk to find him in the cafeteria.

Every day the two of them sat at a different lunch table. Sometimes with the jocks, other times with the geeks, and every once and a while with a crowd of girls. Today Adam sat against the far wall with the learning enrichment crowd, who were taking turns rifling through a computer gaming magazine.

Even though they were best friends, they hardly ever saw each other until lunch. After that, however, they had every class together. They'd made sure of that at the beginning of the school year, just like they always did.

Hacking into the school system and arranging their classes how they liked and with who they liked wasn't hard. Making sure that they didn't make it *too* obvious was the tricky part.

But worth it.

Hill's table at the side of the cafeteria burst into laughter and squeals. Adam looked over to see William Bubert bending over to pick up his glasses. Who knew how many pairs Hill had ruined this year.

Adam looked away.

No, he shouldn't look away. Not after what happened to Tommy. Adam stood and started for the table, but William Bubert was already scurrying away, walking on his toes just like he'd done when they were in kindergarten. William hadn't changed and neither had Hill.

Adam sat back down and pushed his lunch away.

It wasn't hard to stand up for himself or for Perk or for Tommy. It wasn't something that he had to try at or even think about. It just was.

Sure, there were times when he'd help someone get out of a locker or help a kid gather up the books and papers and pencils that Hill had tossed onto the floor.

But most of the time, it was easier to look away.

But this, right here, was the last time.

He and Perk had to come up with some way to get Mr. Parmar and Hill back.

Something they'd never forget. Something that would make up for all the times that Hill and Parmar had stepped, trampled, and steamrollered over someone else.

"So?" Perk said, startling Adam out of his thoughts. "Hey."

Perk plopped down at the table and opened a bag of vinegar chips, stuffing a small handful in his mouth. "You have any ideas? You probably already have a plan figured out, right?"

That was one of the things that Adam liked about Perk. Ever since they were in second grade and Adam had printed off pictures of cockroaches on the school computer during inside recess, Perk had been ready to jump headfirst into whatever Adam had cooked up. He had stepped right in, grabbed a pair of scissors, and cut out each bug with precision, then scooped half of them up. Without a word between them, the two had taken turns with the hall pass, sneaking down to the lunchroom where they placed the paper cockroaches on the cafeteria lunch tables while the school cook was busy with the mushy green beans and lumpy gravy.

They'd smiled at each other after the initial scream and had been best friends ever since. Adam wasn't even sure if they'd ever talked about the prank afterward. They hadn't needed to.

"So?" Perk crunched down on another chip.

How could he eat those things? But then again, Perk was like a garbage can—you put anything in front of him—on a plate or wrapped in packaging— and he'd eat it. Adam looked down at his own lunch, leftover food from the restaurant. He didn't mind it most of the time, and not really even now, but remembering what happened yesterday with Tommy soured his stomach. He scooped up a glob of reheated mashed potatoes, then set down his fork. "Nothing certain yet. Lots of ideas. But this has to be big."

"Agreed. The biggest yet."

Adam nodded. "We're going to need five or six, including us."

"Six?" Perk laughed, shaking his head, then licking the vinegar residue off his fingers. "You're crazy. It's a lot to ask from kids who aren't used to pulling this kind of stuff."

Adam leaned in. Of course, he had wanted it to just be he and Perk. They knew each other and they trusted each other. "Yeah, but doing something huge, just you and me? I'm not sure we can pull it off. It needs to be planned to perfection, and that means more help."

"And if we get caught? More people means more risk."

"You're right—whoever we ask needs to know the risks. That's why we need people who've had run-ins with Hill and his father. And then we need to make sure that whoever agrees keeps everything zipped. If we can guarantee those two things, I don't see any reason why we can't find our crew by this weekend." He took a bite of lukewarm mashed potatoes and swallowed. They went down his throat like glue. "What do you think?"

Perk scrunched up a cellophane wrapper and tossed it at the nearby trash can. It bounced in. "Let's look at some school records."

CHAPTER 4
Perk

Perk waited for Adam on the school stairs nursing a bag of sour gummies, his homework balanced on his knee. He glanced up briefly as Adam's shoe scuffed on the cement, then returned to his homework. Fractions.

Adam dropped down beside Perk and glanced at the paper. He pointed at the problems. "Five-fifteenths or one-third, three-sevenths, and four-fifths."

Perk wrote down the answers and nodded his thanks. "Can't stand fractions."

"My uncle builds houses and fractions are his second language." He reached over and took a few gummies from Perk's open bag and popped them into his mouth.

Perk didn't plan on a career in carpentry. He didn't know what he wanted to do when he was older. Right now his job was school and taking care of Tommy. No, that wasn't right. Taking care of Tommy wasn't a job. He loved Tommy. Tommy needed him.

Perk glanced down at his watch, then stuffed his homework in his backpack and zipped it up. After the other day, Perk wanted to be waiting at the bus stop earlier than on time. Not like it would matter much, but it made him feel better. He stood. "Tommy's bus will be here soon. Then we have Hebrew school. I'll see you tomorrow."

"All right," Adam said. "You think of anyone yet?"

Perk shrugged and started down the walkway. "Maybe a few." He needed to do some research to see if they would really work. Plus, he was still getting used to the thought of other people joining in. But trying to get Adam off an idea once his mind was on it was like trying to get a dog to stop eating a steak dinner.

"Nice. I have a few, too. I'll call you tonight, yeah?"

"Sure."

He was halfway down the walk when Adam called

after him. "Hey, assuming we decide on our crew. Do you think you could make detention tomorrow?"

Perk looked back and dug in his bag for a handful of sour gummies. Adam never got detention, so he probably wanted to make a statement to whomever they found, let them know what the two of them could do. He needed a diversion. Perk's specialty. He nodded. "Tommy has his art class after school tomorrow, so yeah, I can be there."

"Cool. I'll leave the window open—the first one on the right. Let's say three-forty, twenty minutes in."

Perk nodded again and smiled. "How do burritos sound?"

"Perfect."

Perk gave a backward wave and started toward Tommy's bus stop.

He'd only been waiting nine minutes when the yellow bus chugged to a stop, the lights blinking. Perk squinted and looked in the window where Tommy was waving frantically, a wide smile on his face. The knot of fear that had slowly gathered in his stomach released and he waved back, twisting the candy bag closed to preserve the ten red gummies.

He always saved the red ones, Tommy's favorite.

But Perk's stomach knotted back up when he remembered the one day last year when he'd waited at the bus stop with a similar bag of sour gummies in his hand. It had been a frigid, windy afternoon, and thick, wet snowflakes had started to fall. The longer Perk had stood there waiting for Tommy's bus, freezing and wet, the more annoyed he'd gotten. He remembered thinking, Why can't Tommy just walk home by himself for once? Seriously, their house was only two blocks away. Perk had sighed and looked into the bag of gummies that he had bought with his own money. His own money that he'd saved up.

Just red ones had been left. Perk's stomach had growled. For once he'd wanted to eat the whole bag himself. Just once. What was so wrong about that? Besides, Tommy had his own money.

Tommy's bus had chugged down the road toward him.

And Perk had eaten them. All of them. Stuffed them into his mouth, not really taking the time to enjoy their sour sweetness. He had chewed and swallowed them down, then stuffed the empty bag in his pocket just as Tommy had stepped off the bus.

They'd hit like a rock in his gut.

"Did you bring me a snack?" Tommy had asked.

The red sour gummies had already started to eat a hole to Perk's heart. "No. Not today, Tommy. Let's get one at home."

Tommy had looked confused at first. Then he'd smiled and grabbed a hold of Perk's hand. "It's okay, Perk. I'll be okay until we get home."

And Perk had never done it again—not even when he felt like his stomach was going to implode with hunger.

Now Tommy stumbled off the bus, his nose running a little with the cold he'd gotten the other day. "Did you bring me a snack?"

Perk smiled and handed him the bag. "All reds."

That night, after Hebrew school and after playing a start-to-finish game of Monopoly with Tommy, Perk hid away in his room and pulled the Anderson Middle School student records up on his computer screen.

Time to find their crew.

CHAPTER 5
Adam

Adam was almost never surprised.

He'd predicted his surprise birthday parties three years in a row. He had an instinct about when Hill Parmar was standing behind him. And his intuition about people had made them almost predictable.

Almost.

But now, looking at everyone's student file on his computer and finding the scan of the survey that they had all filled out on their first day of eighth grade, Adam was surprised.

The survey was a poor attempt to help teachers "get to know their students better," but for the purpose of picking their crew, it helped Adam more than Mr. Fritz, who didn't even seem to know who was in his class, let alone what their favorite food or their least favorite movie was.

Who would've thought that Lisa Reynolds wanted to be a chef when she was older or that Jonathon McGee's real name was Quincy or that Dutch's legal guardian was his seventy-six-year-old grandpa? But it was Perk, his best friend since second grade, who surprised him the most.

Adam had always assumed that Perk didn't really have a favorite food—after all, he ate anything set in front of him—but on his survey he'd written "eating grilled salmon, roasted potatoes, and asparagus while sitting in a restaurant with my family by the beach."

Adam remembered that meal.

It had been he and his parents who had taken Perk and Tommy to the beach with them two summers ago, not Perk's own parents.

He and Perk and Tommy had spent the week swimming during the day, walking on the boardwalk and eating ice cream in the evenings, and playing games at night until one of them couldn't keep his eyes open. Then, on that last day, Adam's parents had taken them out to eat for one final meal.

Grilled salmon, roasted potatoes, and asparagus.

And it had been delicious.

Perk had eaten every particle on his plate, but that wasn't anything unusual, nor was watching Tommy douse everything on his plate in ketchup.

Sure, Adam and his parents got along better than most kids and their parents, at least from what he always heard. Perk's parents, on the other hand, were pretty absent. They spent most of their days at their respective offices downtown . . . and come to think of it, Adam couldn't even remember what exactly they did. He didn't see them too often, and for that matter, neither did Perk.

That was why Perk was the way he was with Tommy.

And probably why he'd written "with my family" on the survey. And why Adam had put down that he had "two brothers" on his own.

Maybe both of those things were true.

Adam looked down at his list of people. Even though he had pulled the surveys and records up on his screen, those weren't really what he looked at. He'd flipped through last year's yearbook and tried to find people who had two things: motive and talent.

Option one: William Bubert.

Adam knew that he was one of Hill's main targets at school and he seemed to spend more time locked inside lockers or with his underwear wedged between his buttocks than not, so he had motive. Adam didn't know what else, but that could be enough.

Option two: Pearl Wagoner.

Talent and motive. Prettiest girl in school and, according to her survey, was second in the state violin competition last year. Adam didn't care about the violin thing—it wasn't going to help them. She'd dated Hill just a little bit ago, but they'd broken up. Despite the fact that she still hung out with his crowd at lunch, he suspected from the way she rolled her eyes at him or sat as far away from him as she could that there was no love lost. And no one could resist that smile. She'd be the perfect informant.

Option three: Max Lopez.

He wore cowboy boots to school every single day, making him another target for Hill. And though Adam wouldn't have guessed it, he had a knack for poetry. He'd filled out his entire survey in poem format, which was pretty impressive. But, of course, that wouldn't do them any good. Motive would, however, and three bloody noses during the first week back from Christmas break will give you enough motive to last the rest of the school year. Plus he was a cowboy and cowboys are tough, right?

Option four: Ray Richmond.

His round face looked up at Adam from his spot in the yearbook. Ray's grades weren't anything to hang on the fridge. And speaking of refrigerators, Ray was about the size of one, in height and width and probably weight. That was good. He'd be able to lift, push, pull, kick, or knock over anything they needed him to. He was also one of those kids that everyone just sort of forgot about. He was in the background— he never did anything special, and it didn't seem like anything special ever happened to him. Unless you count getting kicked off the wrestling team. He was big, and strong, and overlooked. Most people thought he was dumb, too.

But Adam knew different.

There was that day in science class a few months ago. Their teacher, Mr. Lyman, was lecturing about something that Adam couldn't remember now. What he did remember was watching Ray, who sat by himself at a table across from Adam, take one of the calculators that sat in a box Mr. Lyman had labeled "broken equipment." Ray sat at the table and took apart the calculator and then put it back together again.

"What are you doing?" he remembered asking Ray.

Ray grunted, "Nothing," and kept going.

After class ended, Ray pushed the calculator aside, picked up his pencil—he never brought anything else to class—and left. Adam picked it up, sure that it wouldn't work.

He punched in two plus two on the keyboard.

Four appeared on the screen.

Yeah, Adam wasn't usually surprised and he usually didn't like being surprised.

But there's a first time for everything.

CHAPTER 6
Perk

This wasn't the first time that Perk had looked at all the student files, and it certainly wasn't going to be the last.

When he'd first found a way to access them at the beginning of the school year, it was merely for the challenge of it—though it had proved easier than he had hoped. Then he'd become curious and actually looked at the files of his fellow classmates. And then his curiosity turned into a sort of game. He watched grades roller-coaster and tardies and absences go up as the school year rolled along. A surprising number of eighth graders unfortunately had grandmothers pass away; there were a lot of peanut allergies in the seventh and eighth grades, but the sixth grade had a lot of lactose-intolerant kids. And about seventy-five percent of the students in the entire middle school were either getting braces on, getting braces adjusted, or getting braces off every six weeks or so. He'd never thought of orthodontics as a career choice before, but it was looking like a pretty lucrative business.

In between watching (for the one-millionth time) *Finding Nemo* with Tommy and looking through the files and searching the surveys, Perk came up with three people.

Ray Richmond: He hardly ever missed school, got really good grades in sixth grade yet was barely passing in eighth. But he was big, and if they needed someone strong, he was their man.

Kate Pell, who Perk had had a crush on since first grade, seemed good at science and her mother was one of Tommy's teachers. He didn't really have any other reason to put her name in, but whatever.

Dutch Walker missed school a lot. He was one of Hill's favorite targets and was one of the students whose grandmother had died. Even though his grades were so-so, it seemed like it was only because he did well on tests, since from the look of it he never turned in any of his homework.

Perk sighed and looked over at Tommy, who was laughing at Dory and Marlin meeting Bruce the shark, a bowl of popcorn in his lap.

Even with all the student records and test scores and surveys, no one could really be trusted. Not yet and maybe not ever. After all, if he didn't know Hill and just looked at his student files, he would've thought that he was probably a real decent guy.

It was like the time his parents went to Vegas and came back with five thousand dollars more than they went with. The next time his dad had said, "We're betting big this time."

They came back with ten thousand dollars less than they started with.

This was betting big.

And who knew what they were going to get in the end.

CHAPTER 7
Adam and Perk

"Did you pick anyone?"

"Yeah. You?"

"Yep. Let's read off one at a time."

"Okay."

"Pearl Wagoner?"

Silence. "*The* Pearl Wagoner? The beautiful Pearl Wagoner who was named most promising violinist or something like that?"

"Yep, that's the one."

"No way. She's . . . "

"Just one of the nicest and hottest girls in the middle school? I know. That means she's the perfect informant."

"Are you sure? You know how those popular kids are. She might join in at first but then pull a Benedict Arnold on us."

"I don't think so. I'm putting her down. Who do you have?"

"Dutch Walker."

"Dutch? The skinny kid with the face tic who basically lives inside his locker?"

"Yep."

"That's good. He's got motive. But so does William Bubert. He's on my list."

"William Bubert ratted on me in third grade for selling lollipops at school. Don't you remember? I lost forty-five dollars because of him."

"Dutch Walker it is."

"I also have Kate Pell."

"Conflict of interest."

"What do you mean?"

"You know what I mean. You've liked her since the first day of first grade."

"What about Pearl Wagoner?"

"That's different. I know when I'm out of my league. Besides, my heart only belongs to one."

"Still hung up on Hermione Granger?"

"Still. Now who else?"

"Ray Richmond."

"I picked him, too. I heard Parmar kicked him off the wrestling team."

"Really? Ray would've won the season for them."

"I know. Not very smart."

"You have anyone else?"

"I do, but I think three is enough. You?"

"I think three is too many. So who do we have?"

"Pearl, Ray, and Dutch. You good with that?"

"Yep."

"Then I'll see you tomorrow."

"Tomorrow."

CHAPTER 8

Ray

Ray Richmond was big.

In every sense of the word.

His brother and dad were both big. So was his pappy, and his great grandpappy, and probably all the great-great-great-great grandpappies all the way down the line. If he was descended from Adam and Eve, well then, Adam must've been big, too.

When it was time for relay races in gym class, he was never picked first or second or even before the kid who licked his hands. But for games like red rover and tug-of-war, Ray Richmond was a solid choice.

He'd never been known for his brain. "Wow, that kid looks really smart" was not the first thing you thought to yourself when he walked toward you, and it was the last thing you thought as he walked away.

He'd stopped trying to convince people he was smart a while ago. Besides, what would being smart get him when he grew up and helped his dad run the mechanics shop? When they'd picked their elective courses for high school a week ago, Ray had just opted to join the CAT program and train to be a mechanic.

Force and Motion or the computer class that taught students how to design houses were probably stupid anyway.

His brother and father and pappy didn't think too much of engineering or being smart or getting good grades on tests or doing homework. Ray passed all the tests, never did a lick of homework besides a few science projects that he found interesting, and went from one grade to the next.

And being big had its advantages. He was welcome on all the sports teams that needed a "hefty" kid, and they kept him on the team no matter if he did his homework or not.

Until two days ago, when he was cut from the wrestling team.

Up until then Hill Parmar had stayed clear of Ray Richmond, and Ray had really never noticed Hill except for his loud mouth.

When Hill Parmar joined the wrestling team, Ray found out that in addition to having a loud mouth he was also a bragging, cheating, bullying whiner.

At practice two days ago, they all stood along the mats waiting for their turn to take the center of the ring. Hill laughed and knocked his best friend, Seth, on the arm. "Dude, we missed you the other day after school. You should've seen the look on that retard's face when he couldn't find us." He imitated someone starting to cry.

"So you asked him to play hide-and-seek and then ditched him?"

"Yeah, and it was hilarious, man. Locked him in a room. He started crying. Probably peed his pants. Priceless."

Ray had been to the high school's run-down class-rooms where the special education program was held. He'd helped move some of the old furniture around and stayed to play chess with some of the students.

"You were picking on a disabled kid?" Ray asked Hill.

Hill's eyes shifted and he shrugged. "Yeah, so? You like retards, Ray? Maybe because they're so much like you?"

Like a rubber band, Ray snapped. He twisted Hill's arm behind him, swept his leg, and flattened Hill onto the mat like a pancake on his pappy's ten-inch griddle. Afterward, Ray wondered if he'd set a new record on the amount of time it took him to pin his opponent.

"How's that for priceless?" he whispered in Hill's ear.

Mr. Franco pulled him off.

And then Ray was cut from the team.

"Abusing innocent students in addition to abusing your place in our prestigious sports program is not something that I will tolerate." Mr. Parmar had leaned forward on his desk. "You are no longer a part of the team, Mr. Richmond. In fact, I know the high school coach personally and after I talk to him, you'll be lucky if you ever see a wrestling mat again."

Ray hadn't doubted what he said. He'd heard what Principal Parmar could do. How a few years ago he kept one kid from joining the high school football team and another girl lost a scholarship because of him. Ray didn't know how he did it, but everyone knew that Parmar didn't just hand out detentions, he handed out futures—good and bad.

The principal had stood. "And don't forget about detention. I'll be checking the attendance list, and if you don't show, it'll be an automatic suspension."

Maybe he could've said something. Or maybe he *should've* said something. But in the end, Ray said nothing. He got up and left, not bothering to stop by his gym locker for his clothes.

He wasn't sorry.

His dad would be mad, of course. But he was mad about most things. And Ray figured that if he was really so smart he should've remembered that, if you want to make it through middle school and hopefully high school, you don't mess with Mr. Parmar or Mr. Parmar's son.

Ray had temporarily forgotten.

Now Ray opened his locker, and a note fluttered to the ground. He picked it up.

Sick of being bullied by the Parmars? Please come to detention after school today. Room 207. Food provided. Just come in, sit down, and you'll find out why.

Ray turned the paper over in his hands and then back again.

He knew that handwriting. At the beginning of the year, Ray had made a game of analyzing other kids' writing. He'd been terrible at it at first (who would have guessed that Lisa had horrible handwriting or that Foster had the best cursive he'd ever seen, including his fifth grade teacher's?) But after a while he was able to pick their handwriting out anywhere, whether it was on a bathroom stall, the lunchroom table, a note, or their anonymous votes for eighth-grade class president.

This one was pretty simple: skinny letters and a mixture of print and messy cursive.

But what did Adam Baker want with him?

He was headed for detention anyway.

Only one way to find out.

CHAPTER 9
Pearl

Pearl Wagoner was pretty.

And smart.

And funny.

And kind.

And talented.

Yeah, she had it all.

Pearl didn't remember how she had started going out with Hill Parmar. Of course she'd noticed him because he was good-looking as far as eighth-grade boys go. But he didn't wow her or anything. It just sort of . . . happened.

It must have been in science class, when Hill made her laugh. It was something silly, about a movie that they both had seen and liked. He had imitated one of the characters perfectly. And well, soon after that, she was going out with him.

He'd smiled at her, made her laugh, and seemed to like her, which was more than any of the other boys had done. Heaven forbid a white guy or a black guy like the biracial girl. It was either her friends telling her that so-and-so "isn't allowed to date black girls" or he wasn't asking her out because she was "only half black."

So was she just excited someone finally did like her and that's why she said yes? Sure. It felt good to be liked. Since she'd broken up with Hill, she'd heard a number of boys complain about girls only going out with the cute guys who were jerks. She had gone out with a jerk, she knew that. Besides, she didn't see any guys asking Katie Pell or Andrea Michaels out on a date, and they were both really nice girls with great personalities.

She and Hill had been going out for a week when she'd gone over to his house and had dinner.

Mrs. Parmar petted Pearl's hair. "Wow," she said. "Is the curl natural?"

"Uh, yeah." Pearl stepped back, forced a smile, and smoothed down her hair. It wasn't the first time she'd been asked that and, unfortunately, it probably wouldn't be the last.

"So Pearl," Mr. Parmar had said. "Did you go to the beach over spring break?"

"No," she'd replied, "We just stayed here. We might go this summer, though."

Mr. Parmar took a swig of his water. "How do you stay so tan throughout the year? Hill gets a nice tan during the summer, but during the school year he's pale as a ghost." He chuckled and lightly punched Hill on the shoulder.

Pearl had almost choked on the bite of salad she'd just taken. Was he serious? Everyone at the table—Hill, Mr. Parmar, his mom—continued eating as if the question was as normal as "Is it going to rain today?" Mr. Parmar glanced at her as if waiting for an answer. Hill kept shoveling food into his mouth.

She'd straightened up in her chair. "Actually, I guess you can say that I get it from my dad," she'd said. She laughed at her joke. "He's black and my mom is white."

"Oh, well, isn't that something?" Mr. Parmar said,

taking a swig of his soda. "Black, huh?" He said this more to himself as if to let it sink in.

She nodded. "Yes. Black. And white."

He nudged Hill. "That'll look great on your application to Beaumont this summer. You get it," he said, looking at her and explaining. "An interracial relationship will look good to the committee."

Hill had nodded, "Yeah, cool, huh?" He'd turned to her and smiled like that was normal, expected, a-okay.

She'd gotten a little bit of this before. A white boy in her first-grade class had once called her a zebra, and in sixth grade, a black boy named Ty had said she couldn't have an opinion about the civil rights unit in history because she was only "half."

Her parents had sat her down and tried to help her deal with situations like that, but no matter what, it still made her wonder who she was. Where she fit. If she fit.

But being used so that Hill could get into some camp? She didn't wonder about that. It wasn't going to happen.

She broke up with him the next day.

And three weeks ago, she found her usual report

card of A's and B's littered with two D's and the rest C's.

She'd found herself standing in Mr. Parmar's office.

"This is very disappointing, Pearl," Mr. Parmar had said. "I thought you were a better student than this."

Pearl's face had flushed red. She'd looked down at her report card again, something she had done every few seconds since homeroom, hoping the letters would change. "Something must be wrong," she'd said. "This is impossible. I should have A's in every class, except maybe a B in Spanish."

Mr. Parmar had shrugged. "I don't know what to say, Pearl, but I'm sure you are aware that this prevents you from going to the upcoming violin competition." He turned his back toward her, reaching down for something on his desk.

Pearl's stomach had dropped. That had been her first thought as well. "But we can get this fixed before then, right?"

Mr. Parmar had turned to face her. "I'll try my best, but my plate is pretty full right now with the upcoming teacher reviews."

Pearl, staring at her report card for the millionth time, had looked up. "But we have to."

He waved her away. "I'll see what I can do, Pearl, but I can't make any guarantees." Mr. Parmar had held up his hand to stop her as she'd opened her mouth again and then checked his watch. "Now, I'm sorry to interrupt our conversation but I have to go to a meeting. I'll let you know when things are sorted out." He'd walked to his door and opened it for her.

"But—"

Pearl had been swept out into the hallway, but she turned and looked at the closed door.

She was being punished for breaking up with Hill Parmar. It didn't matter that Hill was late for school every morning, or he bullied half the kids in school, or cheated on almost every single test and piece of homework—he would never see the inside of the detention room. But she was going to miss the violin competition that year.

A few days later, Wednesday, as the end-of-school bell rang, Pearl opened her locker and a note fluttered to the ground. She picked it up.

Sick of being bullied by the Parmars? Please come to detention after school today. Room 207. Food provided. Just come in, sit down, and you'll find out why.

Pearl's eyebrows furrowed and she slipped a piece of gum in her mouth. Was this a joke? She reached for her music folder, then remembered that orchestra practice had been canceled that day for the first time all year. What were the chances of that?

She shrugged and started toward room 207.

Why not?

CHAPTER 10
Dutch

1. Detention
2. Do homework
3. Gramps coming to pick him up
4. Make dinner
5. Play cards
6. Read
7. Go to bed

Dutch had started writing his lists after his grandmother died. Grammie liked lists. Lists of groceries; of flowers, trees, and vegetables she wanted to plant; movies she wanted to see; books she read and wanted to read; things she was thankful for; things she was afraid of; things to remember when she was gone;

things to help Gramps remember since his grandpa wasn't remembering things like he used to.

Dutch's lists were pretty boring but he did it because . . . well, because he hated to think of there not being lists around the house. Also, he hoped that making lists would help his tic—the way he couldn't help but scrunch up his nose and squint his eyes every few minutes, sometimes every few seconds, sometimes every moment. Like now. And now. There it was again.

And again.

Again.

His grandpa said that his tics were getting better, but Dutch couldn't tell a difference. Still, it was nice of Gramps to say. He doubted the lists helped his tic, but they didn't make it worse and that was just as good.

Dutch slunk into his seat in detention and unzipped his coat. It was his grandpa's coat that he used to wear when he was young and spry. That's what Gramps always called himself—spry.

Dutch went to detention most days. Not because he had to go to detention. More because he chose to go to detention. Detention was better than waiting outside for Gramps to remember to pick him up on time.

Waiting outside meant that he was easier for Hill to find.

Besides, he got his work done and then could go home and spend the rest of the afternoon and evening with his grandpa. Hopefully Gramps wasn't too tired to play cards tonight. Hopefully he remembered to pick him up.

Dutch also liked being in the same room with other kids. Sure, he was with other kids in all of his classes during the day, but detention was different. It sort of bonded kids together. And Mrs. Stevenson was nice, for a teacher. She never seemed to mind that he wasn't on the list. She'd just say, "Please tell your grandfather I said hi." And Dutch always did.

"Well, that's very kind of her," he'd say every time.

And it was kind.

Sort of like the note he'd pulled out of his locker. "Please come to detention."

It was nice to be asked "please" from someone other than his grandpa.

Hill Parmar never said "please."

But then again, bullies don't ask if they can bully, which, Dutch figured, was one of the reasons they're bullies in the first place. Dutch couldn't imagine Hill pulling him aside and asking, "Can I please take your school picture because I'm going to Photoshop it on a bikini model and then print off flyers of it and post them all over the school and all over town?" or "I'm going to imitate you when I do my speech for English class and everyone will turn and look at you and then laugh. Is that all right?" or "I wanted to make sure you knew that I just filled your gym shoes and gym shorts with chocolate pudding from the cafeteria" or "I'm going to make a song out of your name that everyone will remember. It goes like this: Dutcha, he isn't worth that mucha."

And he was sure that Principal Parmar would never say, "I'm just going to ignore all the things that my son does to you. Is that all right?"

Dutch pulled out his homework and smiled when Adam walked into the detention classroom.

Adam Baker and his best friend, Perk, had stood up to Hill once before when he'd grabbed Dutch's backpack and then emptied it onto the ground, papers, pencils, books, highlighters, all scattering across the sidewalk and underneath the waiting buses. They told him to stop and then they helped Dutch pick up everything.

Aside from his grandfather, Adam and Perk were the best friends that Dutch had . . . even if they didn't know it.

CHAPTER 11
Adam

"Good afternoon, Mrs. Stevenson," Adam said.

Mrs. Stevenson looked up and smiled, unsuccessfully hiding her romance novel behind an *English and You* textbook.

Adam took a seat on the cold, smooth chair attached to a small kidney-shaped desk. Ray Richmond was already sitting down, overflowing the chair and creaking the strained metal. When Adam and Perk had printed off the detention attendance sheet so they could add in all the new names and take off the other names, Ray had already been listed.

Dutch—the kid with the face tic—squinted and smiled at Adam from his seat two desks in front. Adam grinned back. Now they just needed Pearl.

Adam pulled out his history book and began where he had left off. A few moments later, Pearl walked in and sat down.

Mrs. Stevens put down her book long enough to close the door and take attendance, and then the room fell into relative silence.

At exactly 3:40, Mrs. Stevenson's phone vibrated on the metal desk, jolting her to attention. She glanced down at the message and stood. "I'll be back in a few minutes," she said. "Pearl, I'm putting you in charge. If anyone is caught roaming the halls, I assure you that you will all spend the rest of the year in detention." She stepped out into the hallway and closed the door behind her.

Adam waited until he could no longer hear her shoes, then went to the window.

"What are you doing?" Pearl whispered.

Adam didn't answer. Perk was waiting outside. Just as planned. Right on time.

"Did you put that note in my locker?" Pearl asked. She glanced at the door again, clearly nervous. "You're going to get us all in trouble."

"I got a note, too," Dutch said, holding his up.

"Me, too," Ray said. "What's this about, Baker?"

Adam held up his hands. "I'll explain in a minute." He opened the window, lifted two bags through, and helped Perk inside.

Perk nodded to everyone as he opened the bags and pulled out six burritos, chips, queso, and salsa. "We have about twenty minutes, so dig in."

No one moved.

"What is this?" Pearl asked again, shooting nervous glances toward the door. "I'm not even supposed to be in here, and now you're going to get us all into so much trouble."

Perk unwrapped a burrito and took a bite, then handed a wrapped one to her. "Don't worry, she'll be gone for at least twenty minutes. With commercials, maybe thirty."

When Pearl didn't take the burrito, Perk shrugged and set it back down. "Suit yourself, but they're better warm."

Still Pearl didn't move.

"What do you mean, with commercials?" Ray asked. He walked over and picked up a burrito, then tossed one to Dutch.

"In addition to romance novels," Adam said, holding up the cover of a barely clothed couple embracing dramatically, "Mrs. Stevenson and a few other teachers love a cooking show called *Chop Shop*, which just so happens to be on right now."

"Usually they DVR it, but today the DVR isn't working," Perk added.

"Thanks to you," Adam said.

Perk smiled and bowed.

"Well, that's all wonderful," Pearl said. "But you still haven't answered our question."

"What is all this?" Adam asked. "Like the note said, we're sick of getting bullied by the Parmars and—"

"You want to get them back?" This was the first thing Dutch had said, and it seemed by the way he squinted a few times in a row that he hadn't expected the words to come out.

"Yep, we want to put a stop to it once and for all."

"What are you thinking?" Ray asked. "You have a plan?"

Adam and Perk looked at each other. "We have some ideas," Adam said. "But didn't want to start something until we had enough people. You guys. Each one of you was chosen for a reason. You all have had, at one time or another, a bad experience with our principal, Mr. Parmar, and his son, Hill."

Ray huffed and took a bite of his burrito. "You could say that."

"Whether it has been as one of Hill's punching bags"—Adam looked at Dutch—"or getting kicked off the wrestling team"—directed at Ray—"or not making it to the regional orchestra competition because you dumped Mr. Parmar's son—"

Pearl looked up. "How did you—?"

Perk smiled. "We have our ways."

"Wait," Pearl said. "Believe me, I'd like to get back at Mr. Parmar, too, but I'm not willing to spend the rest of the year in detention just to see them get water dumped on their heads."

Adam nodded. "Fair enough, but not only did we trap Mr. Parmar in his office a few days ago and slather every door in the school with Vaseline, we were able to get into each of your lockers, change the attendance sheet for Mrs. Stevenson, bring food, text Mrs. Stevenson about the show, make sure the DVR was 'broken' to get rid of her, and cancel orchestra practice," Adam said. "If that doesn't show you what can be done, I don't know what else could."

"You guys—?"

They almost had her.

"How are you going to keep us from getting caught?" Ray asked.

Perk took over. "We have three main rules. No one gets hurt, no property is damaged, and we don't get caught. There's always a risk, and whatever we come up with is going to be huge, but if we stick to the plan and everyone keeps their mouths shut, we'll be good."

Adam jumped in. "Still, we understand if any of you don't want to get involved. We'll give you a few days to decide. If you do, come to my house on Sunday. Perk will hand out directions. If you decide this isn't for you, no hard feelings. Just tell us and we'll look for someone else."

"Aren't you going to tell us why *you* want to get back at them?" Pearl asked. "You named all our reasons. What's yours? And his?"

Adam and Perk exchanged glances.

Adam spoke, dipping a chip into the queso. "Hill persuaded Perk's brother, Tommy, to play hide-and-seek after school, then locked him in a utility room with a sign taped to his back that said 'Kick me, I'm retarded.'" Adam crunched down on the chip. "No one gets away with that."

Ray nodded. "I heard about that. Count me in. Whatever it is."

"Me, too," Dutch said.

Pearl looked down at her desk, then nodded. "Where do you live?"

"This is good to hear," Adam said. He handed them each a piece of paper with his address scrawled on it. "We'll talk more on Sunday."

Perk pointed at the clock and gathered up his own trash. "Mrs. Stevenson will be coming back in about a minute. Let's clean this up. We'll see you on Sunday . . . or we won't."

Perk held out the empty bag and everyone stuffed their trash inside before settling back into their seats. Mrs. Stevenson's heels clicked in the hallway. Perk ducked out the window just before the door opened and she stepped in.

"I trust that all went well here," she said, walking over to her desk.

"Yeah. Everything was fine," Pearl said.

The teacher lifted her nose in the air and sniffed. "What's that smell? It smells like some sort of taco."

Adam shrugged and pointed out the partially opened window. "Someone must've walked by with Mexican food," he said.

Mrs. Stevenson eyed them all, then sat down in her chair and opened her book.

CHAPTER 12
Perk

Perk ducked away from the window, crawled along the ground for a few feet, and then stood, carrying the mostly empty bag. He'd bought an extra burrito for Tommy, and Pearl hadn't eaten hers. Score. Reaching in, he pulled out both and looked at the wrappers, leaving the one labeled "no sour cream" inside. It was a nice snack for the walk home. Perk unwrapped the extra burrito and took a bite. Maybe it would help settle his stomach or at least get his mind off the tightening and fluttering inside him.

He didn't feel sick, necessarily, but he felt uneasy. Yes, that was it. Uneasy.

But it wasn't Pearl or Ray or Dutch. He actually felt

better now about them joining than he had before. He was uneasy about them meeting Tommy, but he was always uneasy whenever anyone met his brother for the first time. So it wasn't that, either.

It was himself.

It was the pounding of his heart when he'd knocked on the window and Adam had let him in.

The thoughts that had poked at him.

Will they like the burritos?

Maybe he should've gotten something else?

Was the small yellow mustard mark on his sleeve really noticeable?

Perk took another bite of the burrito and swallowed.

He hadn't worried about what other people thought or even about making friends since . . . since he didn't know when. Maybe it was back in second grade when Adam first met Tommy. Perk hadn't invited Adam home that afternoon. Adam had simply shown up at the front gate. He was grinning like he usually did and held a plate of cookies that his mom had made.

Perk remembered walking up to the security monitor, how his stomach had dropped when he'd seen who it was waiting to come in. Perk and Adam had been friends at school, and they'd even played a few times after school or on the weekends. But never at Perk's house. Now, standing at his door, Adam would expect to come in. Then he'd meet Tommy.

And even then, in second grade, Perk had liked things short and to the point.

It wasn't that he'd been ashamed of Tommy. At the same time, he'd really wanted to stay friends with Adam. *But*, if Adam hadn't been nice to Tommy, then Perk couldn't have been friends with Adam anymore— he *wouldn't* have been friends with him anymore.

Adam had pulled open the door handle. "Hi, Perk. My mom made these. Wow, I like your house."

"Thanks."

Tommy had run out, his red T-shirt covered in chocolate from earlier that morning, but because it was his favorite, he wouldn't take it off until an identical one came out of the laundry.

Perk's mouth had gone dry.

Then Adam had stuck out his hand to Tommy and grinned. "Hey, I'm Adam. Do you like chocolate chip cookies?"

And that was that.

Not until a few days ago, when he and Adam had started trying to find out more about Pearl and Ray and Dutch, did he start thinking about what they'd think of himself.

He knew himself as Tommy's brother. He knew himself as Adam's best friend.

But now he was also just Perk.

What did that mean?

The thought brought a terrifying thrill to his stomach, and he ate the last bite of his burrito.

Was it a bad thing? A good thing? Was it anything at all?

Ray

Ray started down the sidewalk, occasionally glancing down at the directions in his hands. He didn't know how Perk had found out his locker combination, but he couldn't say it surprised him.

Even back in elementary school, that kid seemed to know things. Adam, too. But he'd always known that about Adam Baker, at least ever since fourth grade when he found a way to change the school lunch menu so that every day for a month was pizza day.

That had been a great month.

But did Adam or Perk, Pearl or Dutch or anyone, for that matter, suspect that Ray was smart?

Adam may have thought it for a moment or two at

the beginning of the year.

Ray shouldn't have tried so hard to fix the calculator that one day.

He had taken a strange sort of pride in it, though. He liked fixing things, and when he saw the calculator in the "broken equipment" box in science class he thought he'd give it a try. He'd been so absorbed in it that he hadn't seen Adam watching him until he was almost done.

Then when the bell had rung, he tossed it into the "working" box and walked out without checking to see if he'd actually fixed it.

Adam walked up to him at his locker. "Nice work," he said. "How did you know how to do that?"

Ray had laughed. "It worked?"

"Yeah."

He shrugged. "I was just messing around. Lucky, I guess."

Adam regarded him—and it definitely was more like a *regard* than a *look* or a *glance* or a *stare*. Adam shrugged. "Huh. Seems like more than that."

Ray didn't say anything. Instead, he ignored Adam and walked to his next class.

Adam hadn't said anything like that since.

For a brief moment, when he'd first pulled the piece of paper from his locker that afternoon, Ray thought that maybe Adam suspected that he was more than just muscle and bulk . . . and he'd felt different.

Ray glanced down at the piece of paper with Adam's address and stuffed it into his pocket.

It would take him about fifteen minutes to walk there.

And food was provided.

He'd go.

They probably only needed him because he was big and he was strong. But maybe he'd show them that he was more than that.

Maybe this was his chance to be big and strong and—smart.

CHAPTER 14

Pearl

"Have you done your homework yet?" Pearl's mother glanced up as she pushed fabric through her sewing machine.

"I don't have any."

"Practiced your violin?"

"Just about to."

Her dad was away on a business trip . . . again. He seemed to be taking them more. Maybe if he was home every day, then her parents wouldn't fight as much.

Or maybe they'd fight more.

Pearl pulled out a package of frosted Pop-Tarts from the cabinet, filled up a glass with ice-cold milk, and then started back to her room, balancing the snack and drink on her violin case. Once inside, she gently placed everything on her dresser and closed her bedroom door.

She took out her violin, stroked the bow across the strings a few times, then set it back down on her bed and clicked *Violin Music* on her iPod, the music trilling through the speakers, just loud enough that it would sound as if she were playing.

Of course, she did need to practice, but she couldn't practice *right now*. Not with the crinkled-up slip of paper in her back pocket that told her to go to room 207 for detention. Not after what had just happened about an hour before.

Pearl nibbled on the Pop-Tart then set it down, wishing she'd taken the burrito that had been offered to her in detention. Her phone dinged inside her backpack, and when she pulled it out, three new messages popped up.

KAT: where were u at lunch? Need 2 get 2gether soon. Going 2 sam's right?

SARI: u going 2 sam's on Sat? u should go, don't want 2 b only 1

DELLA: hi! Call me later...john totally likes

u! we need 2 talk! I think u need 2 give him
a chance ;)

Pearl closed her phone and sighed.

If Kat had been listening earlier that morning, she would've remembered that Pearl had a dentist appointment during lunch. And she'd already told Sari two times that she was going to Sam's on Saturday, and she'd already talked to Della about John—how she could never really like him—at least not like that. Besides, wasn't Della the one who told her that John's parents didn't want him to interracially date?

Was anyone ever really listening to anything she said?

And what about Adam and Perk and the others? If she joined in on whatever Adam and Perk were planning, would they listen to her either?

Did she really have anything to say or anything worth listening to?

Pearl broke off a piece of Pop-Tart and popped it into her mouth. Yes, she did have things worth saying and things worth listening to. Maybe she'd be able to prove it if she joined in with Adam and Perk?

Adam. She knew him a little bit. He was nice.

He didn't seem to care what anyone else thought and walked around smiling at everyone—even Hill Parmar—which Hill hated. What wasn't to like about that?

Perk she only knew as Adam's friend. His cheeks usually flushed red whenever anyone talked to him, and he kept pretty quiet. Today during detention was the most she had ever heard him speak. Someone, maybe Kat, had told her once that his brother was sort of a crazy person, but Kat had also told the whole school that Pearl threw up her lunch after she ate it, which was a complete lie, so Kat wasn't the most reliable source.

Ray? He was practically a bully himself. Sari told her that in fifth grade, he put gum in her hair and tripped her on the way to lunch. Pearl never saw that side of him, but with the way he scowled like an angry giant through the halls, she could imagine.

The violin playlist ended, and Pearl reached over to turn it off. She would really have to practice in a minute or two.

But then there was Dutch Walker.

Hill's crowd called him Dutchy Dork. He had a

twitch, or maybe it was a tic, in his face that made him squint every so often—well, more than that. And then there was that old coat he wore Every. Single. Day.

But, there was also third grade.

It had been about five years, and still Pearl had not forgotten that third-grade afternoon. She'd been crying at the end of school, sitting on the bench in front of the school thinking that her mom had completely forgotten about her or that maybe something had happened to her on the drive over. It had been a rainy day, with thick clouds and a light drizzle that slowly began to soak into her purple pants—the ones that she wore Every. Single. Day. The whole day had been terrible. Her best friend, Sari, had shown everyone in the class a note that Pearl had written. Everyone had laughed at the fact that she still slept with her favorite lamb, and her face had burned when everyone tried to get her to hold hands with Chad, who she had said was cute, even though just thinking about holding his hand made her stomach flip so much that she felt like she was going to throw up.

At the end of the day, Sari had said she was sorry, and Pearl had forgiven her.

She was good at forgiving.

But that didn't mean she *forgot*. Forgetting was harder.

She had been sitting on the curb thinking about what had happened when all of a sudden, there was Dutch, kneeling in front of her, not caring that his pants were most likely getting soaked.

He squinted. "Why are you crying?"

"My mom's late. I think she might have forgot." Pearl sniffed and swiped her nose. She wished he would just leave—she didn't want anyone seeing her cry, and she didn't even know him. Maybe he'd tell everyone in school that she'd been crying.

But then again, she didn't want to be all alone, either.

"I'm sure she didn't," he said, squinting again. "But I'll wait with you."

"Did your mom forget you, too?"

Squint, squint. "No. I don't have a mom. Or a dad, actually. Well, I guess I do, sort of." Squint. "My grandpa and grandma. But they didn't forget me. They just run late sometimes."

Pearl nodded.

The drizzle started to pick up, and the cold seemed to seep inside her skin all the way down to her bones and out the other side. She shivered.

"Here," he said. Squint, squint. "You can wear this for now." He didn't hand the coat to her, but instead set it on her head. "So your hair doesn't get wet. My grandma hates it when her hair gets wet."

"I understand." And she did. "Thanks."

"Do you want to hear a joke?"

Pearl shrugged. "Sure."

Dutch got up and sat next to her on the bench. "Knock. Knock."

"Who's there?"

"Old lady." Squint, squint.

"Old lady who?"

"I didn't know you could yodel."

She smiled. "I like that."

And then her mom pulled up to the curb, frazzled and worried and apologizing for being late.

Pearl sighed, relieved. "That's okay." She hopped into the car and waved at Dutch through the slightly foggy window.

After that, she said hi to Dutch every day for the

rest of the year. Sometimes she still did, though she said it so quiet that he didn't hear.

She didn't know why.

But that joke always made her smile.

Her phone dinged.

DELLA: movie on sun afternoon! u in?

Pearl sighed and looked down at the note and then at the directions to Adam's house.

PEARL: sorry, can't. c u tomorrow

Maybe, if she was caught sitting in the pouring rain again, Dutch would tell her another joke.

CHAPTER 15
Dutch

1. Make Pearl smile

2. Join in whatever plan Adam and Perk come up with

When he saw Pearl walk into detention that afternoon, his face squinted again and again and again. He had tried hiding it by popping a piece of gum into his mouth, but it hadn't worked. Nothing ever worked.

And why did he still try to hide it? It wasn't like people didn't know. It wasn't like they couldn't tell. He was the kid that squinted all the time.

He was his tic.

But then Pearl had smiled at him. He'd seen it. It was brief, but it was there.

Sometimes she whispered hello to him in the hall-way. He always heard, but sometimes he acted like he didn't. He didn't know why. Already he was trying to think of a joke to tell her.

Of course he felt bad for Perk's brother and he wanted to get back at Hill, but he couldn't lie and say it wasn't mostly because of Pearl.

"Hey," Adam said after detention. Dutch stood waiting for Gramps to pick him up.

"Hey." Squint.

"You waiting for your dad?"

"Well, my grandpa, but yeah."

"Oh, that's right. Sorry."

"You don't need to be sorry."

Gramps pulled up to the curb, honking the horn twice. He wasn't late today, which meant he'd probably had an afternoon nap. That, along with a good cup of coffee, meant that he'd be ready to play cards this evening.

"Does your friend need a ride?" Gramps asked. He leaned down to see out the passenger-side window, his hat slipping a little off his head.

Dutch didn't really think that Adam would say yes

and get into the car. But then, there they were: he, his grandpa, and Adam riding along down the street. Adam was nice, too. He talked to Dutch's grandpa like he was a real person instead of an old man. Dutch hated when people did that, and so did Gramps. Sometimes, when they were playing cards in the evening, he and Gramps would make up funny things about what people had said to him or to Grammie before she died.

They laughed so hard they cried.

And sometimes Dutch wasn't sure if the tears were funny or if they were for missing Grammie.

They pulled up in front of Adam's house and he opened the door. "Thanks for the ride," Adam said.

"My pleasure."

"I'll see you tomorrow at school, Dutch."

Dutch squinted and said, "See ya."

Adam walked up to his door and disappeared inside.

Gramps pulled away from the curb. "He seems like a good kid."

"Yeah. He invited me to do a project with a few other kids." Dutch hated not telling his grandpa the whole truth, but he also didn't know much about what they were going to do. So maybe it wasn't really a lie.

"That's nice," Gramps said. "How was the rest of your day?"

Dutch left out the parts that had to do with getting locked in the girls' bathroom and not having lunch because Hill had filled his lunch bag with sand. He knew that wasn't telling the whole truth, either, but he couldn't help it. Gramps worried about him. And now, without Grammie around, he seemed to worry more.

And he looked older.

"She was my backbone, the marrow, and the muscles that held me together," he told Dutch when she died.

Dutch wondered if there was much left.

"But don't you worry," Gramps had said. "We'll make it. You and me."

Dutch didn't want to make things harder.

When they pulled up in front of their little apartment building, Dutch hopped out, grabbed the two grocery bags sitting in the trunk, Gramps following after him. Inside, Gramps took off his hat and Dutch took off his coat, then Dutch set to heating up the tomato soup and making the grilled cheese.

Gramps cooked last night, so it was Dutch's turn.

When everything was ready, Dutch took a seat at

the table across from his grandpa and dealt out the cards.

Queen of hearts, king of hearts, ten of hearts, two of spades, jack of diamonds . . . He smiled over the top of his cards, meeting his grandpa's twinkling eyes. Despite Hill filling up his lunch bag with sand earlier that day, Adam and Perk had invited him to join in on a plan to get back at the Parmars, Pearl had smiled at him, he was sitting at the table playing cards with Grandpa, and there was no way that he wasn't going to win this game of gin.

He squinted.

All in all it was a pretty good day.

CHAPTER 16
Adam

He knew he shouldn't.

He really shouldn't.

He wouldn't like it if someone did it to him, right?

But then, would he? He didn't have anything to hide. Besides, everyone was given a school e-mail address that the teachers had them use for assignments and stuff like that, but it wasn't like anyone used it for personal stuff.

At least, he didn't think so.

Adam's cell phone rang and he picked it up. "Hey, Perk. What's up?"

"Hey." He paused. "So I see you're on the school files again."

Adam raised his eyebrows. "You can see what I'm doing?"

"Yep, when you're on this site at least. I can see everything you're doing. And right now, you're snooping around like an old lady."

"Ha-ha. Just looking around for some more info on Pearl and Ray and Dutch. You're not still curious?"

"You know I didn't really want anyone besides us. Are you second-guessing it now? We could still do it on our own if you want."

Even though he couldn't make himself admit it out loud, Adam *was* second-guessing Pearl, Ray, and Dutch. At least a little. What if Perk was right about Pearl and she pulled a Benedict Arnold on them at the end? What if Dutch chickened out? What if Ray messed everything up?

But then how would they be able to pull off something huge just the two of them? True, they'd pulled off their April Fools' pranks, but that was small. Too small. If they decided to do something with Parmar's job, or send him and Hill off to Siberia? That would take more than two.

They needed Pearl, Ray, and Dutch. "I'm not

second-guessing. Just doing a little more recon before Sunday."

"Whatever you say. So what do you want to look at?"

Adam had actually hoped to poke around in their emails a little bit but couldn't bring himself to admit it out loud. That was a borderline "Hill" thing to do. "I don't know. Take a look at their surveys again to see the kind of food they like for tomorrow. Is there anything else that we haven't checked out yet?"

"Let's see. I might have an idea."

Adam watched Perk move the cursor around on the screen. He clicked on a few tabs and opened up Mrs. Fenecky's files.

"The yearbook docs?" Adam asked.

"Why not? There could be something in those. Didn't they do the 'What do you want to be when you grow up?' with all the eighth graders?"

"No, I think that was last year. I think this year was, 'If you could be a dessert, what would you be?'"

Perk laughed. "I can't really see how knowing that Ray pictures himself as an apple pie will help plan a prank, but whatever. At least we'll know what kinds of dessert to get on Sunday."

Adam scrolled through all the files in the yearbook folder. "Here's the eighth-grade baby pictures," he said, and clicked on it. "We can see what everyone's parents said about them."

Perk didn't answer, though Adam heard him crunching down on something on the other end. "I gotta go. Tommy is dying to play Sorry! for the ninetieth time tonight. You'll have to reminisce about the time that you were cute alone."

"Whatever. See ya."

"See ya."

Adam clicked off the phone and first went to see what dessert they thought they were. Perk was right about Ray; he was a piece of apple pie. Pearl, a cinnamon roll, and Dutch was molten lava cake. Perk, of course, was a giant chocolate chip cookie. Adam looked at his, making sure he'd put down "donuts." Check.

He then scrolled down to the file labeled "Eighth-Grade Baby Pictures." He hadn't seen what his parents had uploaded yet. He clicked on his. The picture was one he'd forgotten about. He was all chubby baby fat, sitting on the beach, his hair a curly mess on top of his head and a big toothless grin on his face. It looked like there was drool hanging out of his mouth. Gross. His parents had submitted the caption, "We love you, Adam. We're so proud of the baby you were, the boy that you are, and the man you are becoming." His parents could be cheeseballs when it came to stuff like this, but he still smiled.

Adam moved down and found Dutch's picture. He wasn't a baby, but older, probably in elementary school. He was sitting in an older woman's lap, smiling. Or maybe he was squinting. When did his tic start? Did his grandparents wonder what was happening when they saw him squint over and over again for the first time?

The woman was smiling down at him. Beneath the picture was written, "Your Grammie is looking down in love on you. I love you, too."

It wasn't signed, but it must be from his grandpa.

He continued to scroll until he came to Perk. Perkins Benjamin Irving. He laughed at the tiny version of his friend. It was one of the few pictures that just had him in it. Most of them were with Tommy outside or with Tommy on the couch or with Tommy anywhere, Perk's arm always wrapped around his brother's shoulder. This picture was of just Perk sitting in the grass, a lollipop in his hand and his red hair sticking out everywhere. Underneath the picture were the words, "Mazel tov."

Just then, the cursor moved on its own, down to the same picture, and lingered on the words. Perk was looking at his picture and the caption, too. What did he think of what they'd said? Was he glad that they sent in anything at all? Perk's cursor disappeared from the screen. He'd gotten off.

Adam sighed and found Ray's. He generally thought most babies looked the same and were all generally cute, and Ray was no different. He was chubby and looking at the camera with the surprised expression that most babies have. There wasn't a caption underneath, and Adam cringed when he saw that Ray had actually uploaded his own picture for the yearbook.

Bummer.

Last but not least, Adam went down to the W's and found Pearl's picture. Even as a baby, she was pretty much perfect. Her hair pulled back into two black fuzzy pigtails on her head, her smile wide over perfect baby teeth. Her parents had written, "We love you, Pearl. We can't wait to see what you do and how high you soar. You'll always be our Bear! Love always and forever, Mom and Dad."

Adam closed the files and leaned back in his chair.

There wasn't anything in the pictures or captions that should make him feel any better about asking them to join in on the prank, but for some reason he did feel better. For some reason they were more real now.

And he liked that.

CHAPTER 17
Perk

His heart was in his throat.

Tommy rushed up the walkway to Adam's house and began pushing the doorbell. Tommy loved doorbells . . . a lot. That was probably one of the reasons why Tommy loved trick-or-treating so much—lots of dinging and ringing. Adam was most likely standing just behind the door. He knew how much Tommy liked to ring it, and so he usually waited for the eighth or ninth ring before opening it up.

One, two, three, four, Perk counted, hoping to swallow down the uneasiness that was still creeping up his throat. If anything went wrong with Tommy and one of the others, they'd have to find all new people to help. But then if everything went well with Tommy, he'd be officially friends with them, right? It all hinged on them being kind to Tommy.

Adam opened the door and smiled. "Hey, Tommy. Perk."

"Hey," Perk said. He stepped through the front door into the house that was always just slightly messy—shoes askew, papers stacked on the kitchen counter, family pictures crooked on the refrigerator held up by bright orange Bakers' Place magnets. Perk felt himself relax.

At his house, just before seven-thirty, when his parents usually walked through the door, Perk went from room to room, picking up anything that Tommy had put out of place and stowing away Tommy's evening crafts, a jumble of popsicle sticks, paint, glue, and if he was really unlucky—glitter.

He didn't know why his parents cared so much when they were home so little, but he cleaned up either way.

Adam's house smelled like chocolate chip cookies.

"Hi, Adam," Tommy said. "Did you hear the doorbell?"

"I did."

"I love doorbells." He unzipped his sweatshirt and hung it on one of the hooks by the door. "Hey, it smells like cookies in here. Perk loves cookies. Oh, look, Perk—" Tommy pointed at the table, where there were also cinnamon rolls, apple pie, and, Perk assumed, the molten lava cake that Dutch had put on his survey. Tommy went to the oven. "But is there pizza? Perk said we were gonna have pizza."

"Of course. French fries, too. And my mom bought you both a bag of sour gummies."

"Really? Did you hear that, Perk? Our own bags. But can I have all of your reds? I don't like the yellows. I love the reds. Perk likes the greens."

"Sure," Perk said. He didn't know where Tommy got the idea that he liked the green gummies, but he went along with it.

Adam led the way to the kitchen and handed Tommy the bag of candy and his favorite plate—the white plastic one with a big smiling tomato on the front. Tommy immediately crammed the bag of gummies in his pocket so that his jeans bulged out on one side and then loaded up his plate with food.

Perk hadn't read Adam's survey until last night

when he'd gotten off the phone with him. Nothing surprised him necessarily, maybe the comment about having "two brothers," but Perk had known for a long time that that was how Adam thought of he and Tommy. Still, it was nice to see that Adam had typed it out.

It was funny to think of all the things he hadn't known about his best friend until then, though. Like how his favorite season was fall, and he loved donuts. It was almost like Perk knew both of those things already—Adam always wanted donuts in the morning when they had a sleepover, and he definitely seemed to like fall, but still, Perk had never wondered and never thought to ask.

"You think everyone will come?" Perk asked. He opened the bag of gummies and pulled out a handful, depositing the two reds back in the bag.

"I do."

Perk nodded. "Now we wait?"

Adam shrugged and leaned up against the counter. "Now we wait."

Within minutes the doorbell rang.

Perk looked at Adam, who smiled. "And here we go."

"Are they here, Perk?" Tommy asked. "Are they?"

Perk nodded and grabbed a French fry from off the tray. "Yep. Or at least the first person is here."

Tommy got up and stood by Perk, who wiped off the small blob of ketchup from Tommy's red shirt. Luckily the ketchup blended right in. Not like Perk cared if Tommy was spotless, but still.

The front door squeaked open.

"Hey, Ray," he heard Adam say.

Perk tensed as Ray walked into the kitchen, his eyes first falling onto the food, then to Perk and then to Tommy.

"Hey!" Tommy said, smiling big and wide at Ray. "I know you. You came to Mrs. Pell's room after school. You moved our red couch over so we could fit in the blue chairs. I miss the red couch where it was. Then we played chess. Remember?"

Perk turned to Ray, stunned.

"'Course I remember. Are they going to try and fix up that classroom anymore?" Ray asked, his voice quiet. "They really should."

Tommy shrugged. "I don't know. Do you remember how I won the chess game?"

Ray smiled. "How could I forget?"

"You play chess?" Perk asked.

Ray turned toward Perk. "Yeah, so?"

Perk took a plate and a small step back. "Just wondering."

Ray loaded his plate and put a big blob of ketchup on the side.

"I like ketchup, too," Tommy said. He looked up at Perk, a red blob on his cheek. "Hey, Perk, he likes ketchup, too."

Perk nodded. "Cool."

And it was.

CHAPTER 18
Ray

"Sit here, Ray! Sit here!" It was Tommy. He pointed to the seat across from him.

Ray grabbed his stuffed plate and walked over to the table. Pearl and Dutch had come in within a few minutes of each other and were sitting in the living room with Adam and Perk. They wouldn't start talking about everything until he was there, right?

"Look, I went to Adam's room and got his chess set. We can play, though you better watch out 'cause I might beat you again." Tommy laughed.

"Okay. Try to take it easy on me though." Ray sat down across from Tommy and smiled as Tommy arranged both of their pieces on the board.

"Who went first when we played at my school?" Tommy asked.

"I can't really remember. But you can go ahead." Tommy shrugged and moved one of his black pawns.

"That's nice that Adam let you borrow his chessboard."

"Yeah." Tommy said this in a "Why wouldn't he?" sort of way.

"Are you really close to Adam?" Ray asked. He took a bite of pizza and then made his move on the board. Adam and Perk had obviously done their homework on he, Pearl, and Dutch. It was only fair that he do the same to them.

Tommy looked at where he'd moved his piece. "Adam is like my brother, and me and Perk are like his brothers. I love Adam. Not as much as Perk, but I love him." He moved his bishop and smiled. "Adam says that his house is our house."

"That's cool. Does he ever come over to your house?"

"Yeah." He stopped and moved his rook, taking out one of Ray's pawns. "But only sometimes. Perk says that our house is big and feels empty even though we have a lot of furniture. Do you get to watch cartoons on Saturday?"

Ray moved his bishop and then took another bite of his pizza. "Not usually. My dad and brother always get to decide what we watch." He'd lost count of how many times growing up that he'd wanted to watch cartoons but couldn't because his dad and brother were watching wrestling, a fight, or a car race. He'd never been able to join in the conversations at school about this cartoon or that TV show.

"My mom and dad make me and Perk go to synagogue on Saturday morning even though they don't go except on Rosh Hashanah and Yom Kippur." He took another one of Ray's pawns. He really was a good player.

"But sometimes me and Perk come here and we watch cartoons with Adam." Tommy continued. "But you can't tell."

"I won't." Ray moved his bishop. "That sounds like fun though."

"Yeah." Tommy moved another pawn. "I bet you didn't know that I have a girlfriend."

"I didn't know that," Ray said. He took Tommy's pawn. "What's her name?"

"Her name is Nish. She has long hair and it's brown. We're in love."

"That's really cool."

"Do you have a girlfriend?"

"No." Ray moved a piece, not paying much attention. Ray wasn't any girl's type. He'd known that ever since second grade when he'd told a girl named Cynthia that he thought she was pretty. "Well, I think you're ugly," she'd said back.

He knew that he shouldn't take it very seriously, but things like that weren't easy to forget.

"When I grow up, I'm going to have my own apartment and I'm going to ask Nish to marry me and we'll get a dog because Nish's dog died. Did you know that?"

"I didn't. Is she okay?"

"She still cries at school when she thinks about it. One time she came to school crying because some mean boys were barking and whining like dogs in her face. She cried and told them to stop, but they got louder. Mrs. Pell was reeeeeally mad, but Nish didn't know their names. Sometimes healing from loss takes a long time. That's what Mrs. Pell says."

"Yeah, I'm sure she's right." His fist clenched on his lap. Was it Hill? It didn't matter. Whoever it was would feel his fist on their mouths if he ever found out their name.

"Do you have a dog?" Tommy slid his knight from behind his pawn. Ray's rook was in danger.

"No. But I want to get one someday, too." He moved his rook and lifted his hand, realizing that Tommy's bishop was ready to move in.

Tommy grinned and slid his piece across the board, capturing the rook. "Maybe we can take our dogs to the park together."

"That'd be great."

"What do you want to be when you grow up?"

To anyone else, Ray would've said, "A mechanic." It was what his dad and his pappy and his brother expected. Heck, it was what he expected. But maybe he could tell Tommy what he dreamed of instead. "I'm not exactly sure," he said. "But I want to build and invent things."

"Like Legos?"

Ray smiled. "Sure. That'd be fun, wouldn't it?"

Tommy laughed. "Yeah. I think I want to build and invent things, too."

"Well, then you can come and work with me."

"Okay." He turned to the living room. "Hey, Perk!"

"Yeah?" Perk called back.

"I'm gonna work with Ray when I get older."

Perk smiled and took a sip from his glass. "That sounds great. You guys almost finished with your game?"

Ray nodded. "Probably just a few more minutes."

"Why does Dutch do that with his face?" Tommy pointed over at Dutch sitting on the couch and then squinted his face up a few times, imitating him. "Perk says he can't help it."

"Yeah, that's right."

"There's a boy in my class that does that, too. Maybe they're friends?"

Ray shrugged. He needed to start paying better attention to the board. Tommy was close to getting him into check.

"I know why you're here," Tommy said after Ray had moved a piece.

"Really?"

"Yes. Sometimes Perk and Adam don't think that I'm paying attention to what they're saying but I am."

"I bet you're good at listening."

"My teacher gives me all stars for listening. Sometimes Bobby gets a check mark, and Mrs. Pell has to tell him to settle down and keep his feet still because he likes to move his feet." He tapped his toes underneath the table and the pieces jiggled on the board.

"Why are we here?" Ray asked, hoping to hear more of what they'd said.

"Because some people were mean to me. I thought they were my friends but they're just bullies and you guys are going to help them never do it again."

"You're right." Ray slid his bishop across the board.

"What are you going to do? Check."

"Oh man." Ray moved his king. "I don't know yet." Tommy brought his queen out and Ray knew the game was over. "But whatever we do," Ray continued. "It's going to be what you just did to me."

Tommy looked at him for a moment and then back down at the board. He searched the squares and then clapped. "Checkmate? Did I win?"

"You did." He knocked his king down and held out his hand and shook Tommy's.

Tommy clapped his hands and ran into the living room. "Guess what? I won! I got Ray in checkmate. And you know what Ray said?"

Perk slapped his brother a high five.

"He said you guys were going to do that to the bullies."

"Do what to them?"

Tommy threw his hands in the air. "Put them in checkmate."

CHAPTER 19
Pearl

"Why did the stoplight turn red?"

Silence.

"Because it was caught changing in the street."

Pearl laughed along with the rest of them, Perk turning to explain it to Tommy.

Dutch hadn't said it just for her. He'd said it to the whole group, but he'd glanced quickly at her and squinted like he usually did, and she thought that maybe he did remember that time back in third grade.

Either way, it felt good to smile. It hadn't been the best day, or weekend for that matter, and the laugh felt good.

As soon as her dad had walked into the house from

his trip yesterday, her parents had gotten into some sort of fight. Pearl didn't know what it was about—she had shut her door and taken out her violin, playing the pieces for her upcoming concert fast and furious and so loud that their voices were drowned out.

Songs helped her like that, and when she didn't have to practice pieces for a recital, she played certain songs for different moods.

Right now, sitting with everyone at Adam's house and hearing Dutch's joke, "Hobo's Blues" by Paul Simon played in her head. It was a happy, skipping song that made her forget about her parents fighting. "Hobo's Blues" had turned into her happy song this past Christmas when her parents took her to see *The Music Man* and afterward, even though it was eleven-thirty at night, they went to a diner and each ate their own gigantic cinnamon roll and laughed about something she couldn't even remember.

Last night she would've played "Melodie" from *Orpheus and Eurydice.* It was a slow song and her violin sounded like it was crying. She'd been at Sam's, and Sari noticed she was upset.

"Is everything okay?" she'd asked.

Pearl had shrugged and mentioned that her parents had fought that afternoon.

Since that moment (not quite twenty-four hours ago) she'd gotten five texts from different people telling her that "divorce isn't so bad" or "hope your parents work it out" and "bummer about your parents' divorce." They weren't getting a divorce. Just because they fought sometimes—okay, more than sometimes—it didn't mean divorce.

No, there was still reason for her to be hopeful. Her recital was coming up and her dad would be back from his trip and they would—all three— go together. Maybe they'd even go to the diner afterward.

Her hopeful song was "Spiegel im Spiegel." It wasn't happy sounding but it wasn't sad, either, and made her think of when she'd flown in an airplane for the first time. It was storming and rainy and scary, the plane bouncing everywhere. But then they'd pulled above the clouds and it was sunny. She could see the lightning flashing below, but there was nothing but clear blue out her window.

Pearl's phone buzzed in her pocket and she pulled

it out, keeping it tilted just enough that no one could read over her shoulder.

BECCA: heard about parents. Sorry 2 hear
it. hugs :-)

Of course everyone knew. She shoved it back into her sweatshirt. Who would be the next to get the news? Adam? Dutch? Maybe it would be broadcasted in the morning announcements? *"Pearl Wagoner's parents are fighting more than usual. Please text her your sympathies and advice."*

"So, let's get this prank figured out," Adam said.

Pearl brought her thoughts back to the room. The skipping song had died out and her sad song crescendoed inside her, her fingers on her left hand fluttering silently to the notes she knew by heart.

CHAPTER 20

Dutch

1. Get picked up from Adam's around eight-thirty

2. Play cards (if Gramps wasn't too tired)

His grandpa had given him some jokes before he dropped him off. He always had good ones. "Girls like to laugh," he said. "That's how I landed your Grammie."

Dutch didn't particularly *like-like* Pearl. Well, every guy did, but at the same time, he knew that she was in a different league, one that he couldn't cross into. Pearl, the girl with the perfect brown skin who laughed at his jokes and who had played her violin at the Christmas concert and made it sound like it was laughing or crying or hopping. A guy with a tic doesn't land that kind of girl.

And that was okay.

Dutch told his joke and she'd laughed so hard that tears had pooled in her eyes.

Yeah, she might not ever think of him in the way that he thought of her, but he could make her laugh and that was just as good.

Now, at Adam's house, he glanced at Pearl and noticed something faraway in her look. It was the look that Gramps had when Dutch knew he was thinking of his grandma, picturing her in his head or remembering something she said. Pearl's eyes were fixed on Adam, but he could tell that she was inside herself, miles away where no one could go. Was this how Dutch looked when he thought of things? Things like his grandpa and how he seemed to sleep a lot more than he ever did before. And how there were times that he'd forget something that Dutch knew he would never forget if he was his normal self.

Dutch looked back at Adam and squinted.

Adam continued on. "So now let's talk about the rules." He looked to Perk, who swallowed down a mouthful of chips.

"One," Perk said, "no one gets hurt. Two, no

property gets destroyed. Three, no one leaks. And four—"

"—It's gotta be big." Adam looked around at everyone. "It needs to hit home for Hill and the principal. Any thoughts?"

Silence.

"We should find out what they want. What they love . . . and hate." It was Ray that spoke. Ray, who Dutch had only seen flatten players in football, foul players in basketball, and pin guys to the mat in wrestling. Then again, he was also the guy who had just played a chess game with Perk's brother.

Ray's voice had mumbled toward the end, and by the way his cheeks turned red, Dutch could tell that he had surprised himself as well.

Adam nodded. "That's good. So that means we need to watch them, listen to them." He leaned forward in his chair. "We need to split up. Me and Perk will be on the technology—e-mails, their computers, things like that. But we need people to watch what they do, where they go, and then listen in—conversations, phones, things like that."

"I'll listen in at lunch and keep an eye on Hill,"

Pearl said. "I have a pretty good memory."

Ray shifted a little on the couch. "Parmar's supposed to bring his car to the shop this week. I'll watch and listen."

They all looked at Dutch. He squinted. "It makes sense for me to listen and watch Hill, too. I get a lot of chances."

"Is that okay with you?" Adam asked Dutch. Pearl looked over at him. Heat filled his cheeks.

"It's okay with me. I can take it."

After that, Perk passed out a stack of hall passes to everyone. "Use these as much as you need."

Dutch held the hall passes in his hand.

Five out of five days, he usually spent all his time trying to avoid Hill. He'd found different hallways, cut through the library or auditorium, and even started changing into his gym clothes in a bathroom down the hall—that is, when Hill didn't steal his gym clothes.

Dutch knew what to expect. How long to hold his breath in the toilet. How to get out of a locker, and he had extra pairs of shorts and shirts stored in a maintenance closet. But it was still humiliating. Day after day of humiliating.

It was either reason enough to back out or reason enough to stay in.

Perk offered Dutch a high five. "Don't worry. If you need anything, just talk to me or Adam."

"Thanks." He stuffed the hall passes in his pocket.

He was a part of something.

He was part of a group for the first time.

That was worth a hundred days of humiliation.

CHAPTER 21
Perk

"Mr. Irving," Mrs. DeCampo said. "If you've finished the assignment for today, I hope you're finding something interesting to work on back there?"

Perk glanced up from the computer screen and smiled. "Don't worry about me, Mrs. DeCampo."

She smiled back and nodded from her chair at the front of the classroom.

She was one of the few teachers who seemed to take notice of Perk, more than checking to see if his seat was occupied, so he'd always liked her. Besides, her class, computer lab, which he had on Tuesdays and Thursdays, was where he got all of his most important work done: i.e., changing grades, arranging schedules, reworking the cafeteria lunch menu, reordering stock for the vending machines, things like that.

She had something for them to work on every class, but he always finished the lesson first thing or sometimes before the day it was even assigned (it helped to have access to all of Mrs. DeCampo's homework assignments for the entire year).

He had already finished today's task and so had the whole period to get more information on Principal Parmar. It also helped that today was Tuesday. Mrs. DeCampo never walked up and down the row of students huddled over computers on Tuesdays. Instead, she'd just randomly call out students' names and said that "if they were finished with the assignment she hoped they were finding something interesting to work on." He'd realized this the first month of school. Thursdays were her day to walk up and down the rows for the first ten minutes and the last ten minutes of class.

Because of her bad knees (which she was taking medication for), she was like clockwork.

Perk went back to work and ran the cursor over Mr. Parmar's desktop. The screen was plastered with a big picture of himself next to his car, the 1966 Shelby Cobra that he treated like a baby. Parmar could sometimes be seen during the school day wiping the sleek side with a piece of cloth or rushing outside to chase away a group of robins sitting on a wire above the car.

Come to think of it, Perk hadn't seen that telephone wire recently. That's probably what the electricians were doing a few months ago.

He shook his head and clicked on Mr. Parmar's e-mail. There were a few messages back and forth with the director of a place called Camp Beaumont, a few on cars and car shows and taking care of your car and the value of your car and everything else about your car.

Gold.

This was going to be more fun than he had thought.

CHAPTER 22
Adam

Adam grinned as the screen name—Hillisawesome—
popped up on his computer. Well, he guessed it was
really Hill's computer . . . on his computer. It was confusing, but Perk had set it up and all that Adam got was
that now he had Hill's desktop, complete with a picture of Hill flexing his muscles, on his computer. He
had to be careful not to make it obvious to Hill that he
was being hacked, but he figured he was relatively safe
since Hill didn't notice too much of anything.

Adam could've waited until the evening to open up
his laptop and get to work, but he was too excited.
Instead, he brought his computer to the restaurant so
that he could look at it during his break. He'd waited

for a lull in the rush, and when his mom gave him the go-ahead, he stepped into his parents' office.

"Fifteen minutes," she'd said.

Adam laughed again at the screen in front of him. In addition to the picture of Hill and the screen name, which were priceless, Adam found a few stories Hill had written about a squirrel named Bing Bing who tricks the other squirrels out of their acorns and eventually makes his way to the top of the tree and becomes squirrel president.

Then there were the papers.

An English paper due next week that still had Philip Tan's name at the top.

A social studies paper on propaganda during the Hitler regime written by Dutch. Adam could tell because of the lists. It had probably taken Hill longer to turn the lists into an actual paper than if he had just written it himself.

He thought about Dutch and the way he had looked at Pearl the other night. It was obvious that he liked her. And it almost seemed, with the way she blushed, that she liked him, too.

Adam's mom popped her head inside the office.

"You have about five more minutes, okay? It's starting to pick up out here."

Adam nodded. "Sure thing."

Five minutes was enough.

When the door closed, Adam clicked on a file labeled Book Reports. Inside were written book reports on pretty much every book that the students had to read in eighth grade.

Adam dragged all the files into the trash and hit Empty.

It was the right thing to do.

He clicked on another file that had information on a camp called Camp Beaumont, "a camp for only the most prestigious students who excel in academics, deportment, chivalry, and athletics."

Adam smiled and left the brochure open. He went to Hill's e-mail and e-mailed himself the file, then covered his tracks by deleting the message from the Sent box. You never knew when Hill's camp on chivalry, deportment, and excellence in academics would come in handy.

Adam scrolled through the e-mails just as a new message arrived in Hill's in-box from Devin

Howell—a kid Adam had found stuffed inside a locker once. It was a book report.

To delete or not to delete? That was the question.

Adam was just about to drag the file into the trash when he realized that Devin might be spending more time stuffed inside his locker tomorrow if Hill didn't get the report.

He let it go.

Three minutes.

One of Adam's favorite discoveries was a love e-mail that Hill had sent to three different girls he had apparently met at a Camp Beaumont informational meeting a month ago. It included things like "I can't get you out of my mind," "I'm hoping to help out with my local animal shelter this summer," and "I can't wait to see you."

The only thing that he'd bothered to change were their names.

Priceless.

Adam glanced up at the clock. His break was over.

But before he closed down, he forwarded the e-mail to himself and then onto Michelle, Natalie, and Gigi so that they could all see what Hill was doing.

It was the right thing to do.

CHAPTER 23
Ray

Wax on.

Wax off.

Unfortunately, this wasn't that old Karate Kid movie he'd seen on TV, and he wasn't being taught by a Japanese karate expert, and he wasn't going to get the car in the end or the girl. But, he supposed, in a way, he was learning how to get back at Parmar and Hill one swipe at a time.

Ray didn't mind waxing the cars that went through his dad's shop. It gave him time to think about stuff and he was good at it. The bonus was that for a few hours his dad, his pappy, and his brother left him alone.

"Make sure you're thorough," Mr. Parmar had said. "I don't want a spot on it."

Ray nodded and swiped at a panel that he'd already wiped five times already.

He had Mr. Parmar's precious 1966 Shelby Cobra under the rag in his hand, and it was taking everything in him to keep himself from scratching off some of that shiny red paint.

Unfortunately, he hadn't learned too much about Parmar by waxing his car. The principal loved his car, but Ray had known that for a while; everyone did. You could hardly walk by the car and breathe without Mr. Parmar rushing out and yelling at you for getting too close or swiping off the carbon dioxide that you dared to emit around the car. From the looks of the inside, he kept it pretty immaculate, too, except for a few Snickers bar wrappers.

Maybe that could come in handy.

Mr. Parmar, who had insisted on watching him wax the car in case Ray "treated his car like he did his wrestling teammates," now reached for his phone.

Wax on.

Wax off.

He dialed a number.

Ray listened in.

"Hello, this is Bill Parmar. Can I speak with Mike please? Yes. Oh, hello, Cheryl." He rolled his eyes and listened for a moment or two. "Well, the classroom isn't that bad. I know you're underfunded, but aren't we all? Besides, I don't have anything to do with the budget, that's Mike and the other board members. Sure, it could use some renovations, but really, I think our money is best spent on the students who actually—"

Pause.

"Now, I didn't say your students aren't important. But they're different, and maybe we can help them in different ways."

Pause.

"I know my budget requests for the sports teams weren't originally in the plan, but I can't help it if the board decided—"

Pause.

"I didn't persuade anyone. Well, we can talk about this later. I'm on a tight schedule, so if you would please just get Mike. I will. Why don't you stop by my office this time."

Mr. Parmar heaved a sigh. "Hi, Mike. Cheryl's on a roll today. Her contract isn't up yet, is it?" Pause. "I know. Well, look. I called because Hill is going to a camp this summer. It would be great for his application if he could have some volunteer hours logged in. Helping out at the special needs program would look great. Yes, I know it's late in the year, but I—"

Mr. Parmar glanced over at Ray, pointed, and whispered, "It looks like you missed a spot" before continuing. "I was hoping that we could make another arrangement. Yes. I see that your daughter Amanda is doing well in school. That's wonderful. But I'm sure you'd like her to do better, and you certainly wouldn't want her to do worse, especially when we're arranging high school placement classes right now? Yeah. No. English? I think that could happen. Hey, I appreciate it. Why don't you send it to my office. Thanks, Mike, and congratulations to Amanda."

Click.

His phone immediately began ringing.

"Hello, this is Bill Parmar." Pause. "Oh, Mr. Braynard. Very nice to hear from you."

The difference in his voice was obvious and Ray

swiped across the side of the door, stepping closer to where Parmar stood so that he could hear better.

"No, we have not finished the application for Camp Beaumont yet, though I know that Hill is working on it. Taking his time, wanting everything to be perfect. You know how it can be with these overachieving kids." Pause. "I understand. We will get that sent out by the end of this week. When would you like the video interview completed?" Pause. "I'll have him start working on it right away." Pause. "I understand. Thank you. We look forward to this summer as well. Good-bye."

Mr. Parmar shoved his phone into his pocket, turning to Ray. "You done yet?" He looked up at the clouds gathering in the sky. "I don't like to drive this beauty in the rain."

Ray swiped, pretended he saw a speck, and swiped one more time. He stood up. "Done."

Mr. Parmar inspected the sleek body of the car. He looked it all over, trying to find something wrong, but he wouldn't. Ray was good at waxing, better than his brother and almost as good as his dad. He'd practically grown up with a rag in his hand and knew how to change oil before he could walk. Mr. Parmar grunted and then walked inside to pay.

Ray's pappy limped out with the keys and eased himself into the front seat. "Good job," he said, his voice raspy and his bottom lip stuffed with chew. "Almost as good as your dad, though not quite."

Ray nodded his thanks at the rare sort-of compliment and tucked the rag inside his jeans pocket as his pappy drove the car to the front of the shop.

A minute later, there was the screech of tires as Parmar pulled out and zoomed to the intersection.

Ray pulled out a small spiral notebook and wrote four things down: Parmar's obsession with his car, Hill volunteering with the special education class at the high school, budget and funding, and Hill having to fill out some application and creating a video to get into some sort of . . . something.

That last one especially could be valuable.

"Ray," his dad called. "You got another wax around back."

"All right."

CHAPTER 24

Pearl

Sitting at the lunch table with Hill Parmar was as torturous as listening to her little cousin, Suzanne, try to play the violin.

Her cousin was cute, but the screeching and scratching of her bow on the strings made Pearl's skin crawl. Hill wasn't bad to look at, but when he opened his mouth it was like listening to the screech of "Away in a Manger."

She doubted whether Adam, Perk, Ray, or Dutch knew what they were putting her through.

Still, she needed to do her part.

And then there were Sari and Megan and Lilah and Della and Star all cooing and oohing and ahhing and giggling at every stupid thing that Hill said.

The greatest struggle she had was acting like she was interested.

Pearl glanced over at Adam and Perk sitting at a small table by the window. They ate—or at least Perk did—and talked about something. She spotted Dutch standing in the cafeteria line chatting with the lunch lady. The old woman laughed. Maybe Dutch was telling her a joke.

Pearl wished she could hear what he was saying.

She didn't feel like she was learning anything about Hill or Mr. Parmar that would help besides the fact that they were both arrogant and treated everyone like something they could step on if they wanted.

But that wasn't anything new.

"So yeah, I'm going to this camp in Massachusetts that's, like, the best camp out there. Anyone who's anyone goes there. It's gonna be sweet."

Pearl turned her attention back to the lunch table.

"When do you leave?" Sari asked, pouting a little.

Hill shrugged. "It's, like, all summer long, so right after school ends."

"Is that the camp where those girls are going—the

ones who sent those break-up e-mails to you last night?" This was from Seth, who Pearl could tell had a huge crush on Sari.

Pearl's friends tensed at the mention of "those girls."

Hill broke in suddenly. "Just some chicks I met at the informational meeting. But you don't know what you're talking about, Seth. I broke up with them. Don't want anything tying me down, you know what I mean?" He winked at Sari.

"It's Camp Beaumont, right?" This came from one of Hill's other minions, Chaz. "I heard you have to apply to get in there. Have you done your interview?"

Hill shot him an annoyed look. "Yeah, like I even need to apply. My dad talked to the camp director yesterday after school. They're going to make sure that I'm in a good cabin. I don't have anything to worry about."

Seth nodded. "Cool."

"Hey," Hill said, and nudged Seth with his elbow. "You should see the posters I made for the spring dance." He unzipped his backpack and showed Seth a stack of papers.

Seth laughed. "Priceless, man. When do you want to hang them up?"

"Tomorrow morning. You in?"

"Sure."

"Can we see?" Megan asked.

Hill zipped his backpack closed. "Not yet, but don't worry, you will."

"So," Megan said. She twirled a curl around her finger. "Who are you going with?"

Pearl sighed and took a bite of her sandwich.

Screech, screech, screech.

Torture.

CHAPTER 25

Dutch

1. Use one of the hall passes

2. Go around and take down as many pictures hanging up as I can

3. Try not to care

Dutch knew that most of the school had already seen the posters—you couldn't *not*. The teachers had tried taking them down, but as quickly as they tossed them in the garbage, three more would appear over the next period. Besides, you couldn't forget his face plastered on a poster with the words, "Elect Me for Spring Dance Dutch Dork!"

And he wished that the people who had seen the posters would forget about them as easily as Gramps forgot where his bedroom was or that Grammie was not still alive or that he needed to pick Dutch up from school.

But wishing the posters had never been taped up was pointless, and so was ripping a poster down and crumpling it in his fist. Still, that made him feel like he was doing something.

Who cared about the posters anyway?

It wasn't like he was going to the dance, it wasn't like he was going to ask anyone, it wasn't like anyone would say yes if he did.

Pearl wouldn't.

He walked into the boys' bathroom and took the posters taped above the sink and then each one that hung above a urinal or a toilet. He thought of flushing them but couldn't bring himself to do that to Mr. Jelepy.

It wasn't Mr. Jelepy's fault that Dutch was a dork.

His grandma had called him brave but she was the only one who ever had.

Dutch stopped in front of the mirror and looked at himself. His dark hair and dark skin and dark eyes. His constantly squinting eyes and mouth and the way the vein on his neck would stick out a little bit every time reminded him of a lizard.

A dorky lizard.

A dorky lizard who would most likely win King Dork of the spring dance.

And then the dork that stared back at him from the mirror heaved in a shaky breath and let a tear escape through his squinting eyes.

Just then the bathroom door squeaked open, and Dutch ducked his head and swiped his hand across his eyes.

"Hey, Dutch." It was Adam. He had a handful of posters that he quickly shoved into the trash can, as if Dutch didn't know what they were. "I thought I saw you."

"Oh . . . hey." Dutch looked down at the sink and turned on the water, washing his hands even though he hadn't gone to the bathroom. "It's okay, you know."

"Huh?"

Dutch pointed to the trash can. "The posters. I'm used to it." But he wasn't used to it. He should be, right? He looked at himself in the mirror again. At least his squinty eyes weren't red.

Adam looked in the mirror—his eyes and mouth and face normal and perfect and unmoving unless he *made* his face move. He saw Dutch watching him and turned, leaning his back against the sink. "What do you say we get him back?"

"What do you mean? Aren't we already doing that?"

"Yeah, but we could do a little something today, or tomorrow maybe. Like practice."

Dutch shook his head. "Don't worry about it," he said. "I can handle it."

What else could he do?

Adam stood up straight. "It's not because of the posters," he said. "Even though Hill was bragging in science class that he has more stashed in his locker. Practice is a good idea."

Dutch shrugged. Hill had more posters? "Well, if you want to." He grabbed a paper towel and dried his hands. "I'm in for whatever."

Adam followed him out of the bathroom. "I'll let you know what we come up with."

"Thanks."

"Sure."

Dutch started back down the hall to his class when

Adam stopped him. "Hey, Dutch?"

"Yeah?"

"How about we take the rest of these down?"

Dutch grinned.

Adam nodded. "Let's start in the cafeteria."

CHAPTER 26
Adam

Adam slid onto the bench seat next to Perk, his paper bag lunch partially squashed from when he accidentally tossed his math book on top of it in his locker. "Hey."

"Hey."

"Did you see them?"

Perk looked up and took another bite. "What?" he asked, his cheek round and full. "The posters?"

"Yeah."

He nodded and swallowed. "They're everywhere. Hill is not creative, but I'm impressed that he was so thorough."

Adam agreed and pulled out his flattened sandwich

and bag of chips that were more crumbs than actual chips now. "Dutch was pretty upset. I saw him in the bathroom."

"I can imagine."

They were silent for a moment, Perk starting in on his second plate of lunch and Adam trying to enjoy his warm, smooshed tuna fish. It wasn't easy. He couldn't forget Dutch's face in the bathroom mirror. His eyes filling up to almost-overflowing, his face cast down as soon as Adam walked in.

Perk broke the silence. "We're doing something about this, right?"

Adam didn't say anything. The cogs and wheels in his mind clicked and turned.

Perk continued. "Something a little smaller than what we're going to do in a few weeks? Maybe something to test us as a team?"

Adam was still silent. Put Hill's face on a poster and hang them all over the school? No, that wasn't good enough. Ideas fired around, but none of them seemed to hit the target.

Lunch ended and everyone threw their trash away and headed to class. Perk knocked Adam on the arm.

"We'll figure it out. See you after school."

"Yeah," Adam said, distracted. "After school."

The last place he thought he'd get an idea from was his PE teacher, Mr. Franco.

Mr. Franco didn't usually lead or guide or help Adam, at least not on purpose, unless it was to go faster, jump higher, throw farther, or kick straighter.

But sometimes ideas come from unexpected places.

"Baker," Mr. Franco yelled out. "Reach. Reach! You're never going to get flexible if you don't do something today, now, this moment." He circled the group of boys hunkered over their legs. "If you're not going to give it your all, then take your things back to your locker and throw away the key."

Adam was struck with inspiration.

After the last bell, Adam stopped by Perk's locker. "I've got it," he said.

Perk nodded. "I have to meet Tommy's bus, but call me later."

And later it was all set.

CHAPTER 27
Perk

If Pearl was right, Hill should be in the bathroom right now.

"He brags that he only uses the teachers' restroom," she'd said. "He's in my science class and every single day—seriously, he's like clockwork—he takes the hall pass and goes to the bathroom about ten minutes before the end of class."

Perk stood by his locker and glanced down the hallway. Where was Adam?

Just then his best friend came jogging around the corner, a plastic bag in his hand.

"Sorry," he said, handing Perk the bag. "Mr. Gutierrez was feeling a little stingy with the hall pass today."

Perk took the bag and looked inside at the rope, sign, and tape. He started toward the teachers' bathroom. "No worries. Is he in there?"

Adam nodded. "I just saw him go in, so hurry."

"Got it," Perk said, smiling. "Wish me luck."

He turned the corner, ran down the hallway to the bathroom, then pressed his ear against the door. The toilet flushed.

The door couldn't lock from the outside without a key, but he could definitely keep Hill inside for a while. He wound the rope around the handle and then pulled it taught just around the corner, winding it around the fire extinguisher box. He tied a knot and then pulled tighter.

The sink was running now.

Perk giggled to himself and tried to move faster; his heart was speeding up and his hands were sliding with sweat. He grabbed the sign that read "OUT OF ORDER. DO NOT OPEN" from the bag and taped it to the door just as the handle pulled down and Hill tugged.

"What the—?" a voice said.

Perfect.

He covered his mouth, suppressing a giggle, and

then walked back down the hallway, stuffing the plastic bag into the trash can.

He didn't know how long it would take for someone to hear Hill and then get him out.

Hopefully Pearl, Ray, and Dutch were moving fast.

CHAPTER 28
Ray

Seven minutes.

Ray knew which gym locker was Hill's.

Probably everyone knew.

All anyone needed to do was listen to Hill brag on and on about it.

He was number 1.

Ray slipped Mr. Vinnzeli's hall pass into his pocket and pushed the locker room door open. He walked up to Hill's locker and took out the new combination lock that Adam had given him that morning.

"You have the lock cutter?" Adam had asked.

Ray nodded, even though he didn't. His dad had

a lock cutter at the garage, probably several, but Ray hadn't brought it.

His reasons?

Number one: His dad would find out, and that was worse than Hill realizing Ray had broken into his locker.

Number two: He didn't need a lock cutter.

Ray had learned how to open a combination lock without the combination a few years ago. He'd seen a movie about a group of guys who were robbing a bank. One of the men stood near the vault lock and listened for a small "click" as he turned the dial. Ray had assumed that combination locks were similar.

They were.

He'd practiced for months and months and gotten pretty good at it. It had been a while since he'd last opened one, so he might be a little rusty. Hopefully not longer-than-seven-minutes rusty.

He held the lock in his hand and slowly turned it clockwise. Thirty-four.

Counterclockwise. Listen.

"Click." Forty-six.

Clockwise.

The third number was the hardest number to decipher because as he turned the dial, the whole thing seemed to click. When it became harder to turn, he pulled down on the lock shaft.

Perfect.

Thirty-four.

Forty-six.

One.

Ray smiled and stuffed Hill's gym clothes in an empty locker. Then he put the new lock on Hill's locker, walked out, and headed back to class.

"And where have you been, Mr. Richmond?" his teacher asked.

Ray hung the hall pass on the side of the door where it was kept. "Just taking care of business."

CHAPTER 29
Pearl

Five minutes.

Pearl grabbed the other hall pass from the door and walked into the hall.

Her heart double-timed in her chest, and she wiped her palms on her jeans. Fast, high-pitched violin music played in the background of her mind. She had five minutes to open Hill's locker, and then Dutch was supposed to pass her in the hall and slip a new lock on.

"I'm sure we could all do this prank on our own if we wanted," Adam had said. "But let's see if we can get out of class and work together to get it done. Timing is everything."

"And not getting caught," Perk had replied.

"Yes, and that. Pearl, you're sure you remember his locker combination?"

"Yeah."

Or, at least she was pretty sure she remembered.

If she remembered the combination, she'd be done in thirty seconds.

She found Hill's locker and stood in front of the lock. She closed her eyes.

Twenty-two.

Five.

Thirteen.

She saw the numbers clear as a high C in her head, written down in Hill's writing. He'd given it to her, writing it on the back of a paper she'd written for social studies.

"Just in case you ever want to do something special for me," he'd said.

She should've gotten the clue right then.

Pearl opened her eyes and twisted the dial clockwise, then counterclockwise, then clockwise again.

Click.

She grinned.

After taking off the lock and tossing it into the

nearby trash can, she started back to science class.

Just before she reached her classroom, Dutch slipped out of Mrs. Henderson's classroom. She had language arts with Mrs. Henderson, too, except during sixth period.

He looked at her and smiled. Or maybe he just squinted, she couldn't tell. It was sort of cute.

"Did you get it?" he whispered.

She nodded and ducked back into her classroom, glancing back to see him disappear down the hall.

Was she weird for thinking that he was cute?

Did she care that it was weird?

CHAPTER 30
Dutch

Three minutes.

He'd never done something like this.

He couldn't mess it up. It was simple enough that he really couldn't, unless for some reason, someone caught him.

What if Pearl had shaken her head no and he just thought it was a nod because his face was ticking so much. No, he had to focus, to pull out the new lock and put it on Hill's locker.

They were counting on him.

He looked up at the clock.

Two minutes.

But before Dutch put the new lock on Hill's locker,

he opened it. He had to. Amidst a cluttered mess of papers and books, Hill's jacket and backpack, was another stack of posters with Dutch's face plastered on them.

Dutch's hand was steadier now. His face wasn't squinting as much. He grabbed the stack of papers and tossed them into the trash can. Then he snapped the new lock on the door.

A knot that had formed—hard and tangled—in his chest released. As he dashed back to his class, he glanced in at Pearl's classroom and caught her eye.

She smiled.

He smiled, or squinted.

He wasn't sure which.

CHAPTER 31
Adam

Hill was stuck in the bathroom for almost all of fourth period, couldn't open either of his lockers for the rest of the day, and no one was caught.

Their plan was a success.

"What do you say that we all go to the restaurant after school?" Adam asked Perk. "You know, keep planning and celebrate."

Perk nodded. "Sure. I can see if Mrs. Miller can pick up Tommy and watch him for a while."

Adam liked Mrs. Miller, Tommy's sometime baby-sitter, too. She smelled like warm bread and looked like a human version of a golden retriever, but still, Adam was surprised that Perk wouldn't want Tommy to come. "You know he can come, right?"

"Sure. It's just . . ." Perk shrugged. "You know how he is; sometimes he's not good at keeping secrets. And if we're planning out what we're going to do, it'll just be easier."

"Maybe. Well, if you see anyone, let them know and I'll do the same."

"Sure."

Thirty minutes after school ended, Adam watched and waited behind the counter at Bakers' Place.

He jumped up from his stool when they all pushed through the entrance, laughing. "Hey, come on in, guys!" he called. "Let me just tell my mom you guys are here. Where's Perk?"

"He said he'd be a few minutes late. He had to get Tommy off the bus and meet the babysitter."

"All right." Adam ducked into the back and peeked his head into his parents' office. "My friends are here, so we're gonna sit down at table seven. Is that okay?"

His mom licked an envelope and smiled. "Sure."

"Thanks." Adam grabbed a stack of dessert menus and strolled out.

Let the plotting begin.

CHAPTER 32
Perk

Tommy was fine. He liked Mrs. Miller.

Sure, he wasn't happy when she met them at the house, but Perk just couldn't bring him along today.

And when Perk got home, Tommy would probably not talk to him for the rest of the night when he found out that Perk went to Bakers' Place without him, but it wasn't something that Perk could help. Not this time. If they were going to do something huge, they needed to get moving.

Perk kicked a stone.

He loved his brother. Of course he did. He loved him more than anyone else.

Was it awful of him to want to go to school because

it sometimes felt more relaxing than being at home? Was he a horrible brother because he liked the idea of being just Perk for a little bit? That he wanted to have his own friends and not constantly worry about Tommy?

No, he couldn't think like that.

He'd do anything for Tommy.

Then why is he with Mrs. Miller and not you?

Perk stuffed the thought away. It wasn't like that. Besides, he needed to think about a plan to get back at Hill and his dad.

Yes, that's what he needed to think about right now.

Something with the summer camp Hill wanted to go to?

Perk pulled open the door to Bakers' Place.

"Hey, Perk," Adam called. "Over here. I already ordered your monster cookie."

Perk grinned and walked over to the table and sat down. "Thanks. Sorry I'm a little late."

He sat down and felt like something was missing. Maybe he should've brought Tommy along after all? The thought tugged on his sleeve and tapped on his shoulder even after he took a giant gulp of water.

CHAPTER 33
Adam

Adam blew a few bubbles into his chocolate milk then looked up. His fingers twitched in excitement. Mary—Adam's favorite waitress—had just set down their desserts, and it was time to get started. "So, everyone," he said. "What have you found out?"

They were quiet for a moment, looking around at one another, no one wanting to go first. He could tell his best friend was distracted. Probably thinking about Tommy. Probably wondering why in the world he hadn't invited him. But maybe he was right. They couldn't afford anyone finding out about the plan, and if there was any chance that Tommy might say something, anything . . . well, they just couldn't take that risk. "Perk, anything interesting in the e-mails or on Parmar's computer?"

Perk swallowed a sticky bite of chocolate. "Well, Parmar had a lot of e-mails about cars, which isn't too surprising, and some things on a camp for Hill this summer."

"Hill's talked about that camp at the lunch table," Pearl said. "He was saying that his dad can pretty much get him in and that it's a really good camp, blah, blah, blah. That's all."

Adam nodded. "I think we're on to something. Hill had the brochure of the camp on his computer. Camp Beaumont, I think it was called."

"Yeah," Ray said. He took a gulp of water. "I heard Parmar talking to someone—sounded like a teacher, maybe—about getting Hill volunteer hours in Tommy's after school program for a camp."

"At the high school?" Pearl cut in. "I just found out that me and a few others from the orchestra are going there after school tomorrow to play a few songs. I bet he's going with us." She rolled her eyes and shook her head.

"That jerk shouldn't be anywhere near Tommy's

class." Perk stabbed at his chocolate chip cookie.

"But at least I'll see Tommy," Pearl said. "I'll make sure I say hi."

Perk stuffed a bite in his mouth. "Thanks. He'd love that."

"And it could be a good chance to get more info on Hill." Adam turned back to Ray. "Did Parmar say anything else?"

Ray swallowed a bite. "Yeah, something about Hill turning in a video of himself."

Adam looked up. This kept getting better and better. "A video? Awesome."

"Yeah," Dutch said. He took a bite of his lava cake. "I'd love to see that."

Adam was impressed. With their little prank earlier and now this, he was feeling better—like they could pull off something really cool. He looked at Perk, who nodded back at him.

"All right," Adam said. "Now, anyone find anything else about Parmar besides his obsession with his car and making sure Hill gets into this camp?"

Dutch squinted. "Do we need anything else?"

Adam nodded. He had a point.

CHAPTER 34
Perk

It was nice that Parmar and Hill were so easily predictable. A few conversations and some e-mails and
they already had a direction to go in. Camp and car.
He looked over at Adam. His best friend had the same
frantic, excited look on his face that he got every time
they were thinking of pranks to pull. In a minute he'd
be steamrollering ideas over everyone. Perk needed to
step in and give the others a chance.

"Does anyone have any ideas of what we could do
with the camp and the car?"

Adam stood, his chair screeching beneath him. "I'll
be back. I'm just going to run and get my computer. I
have a thought."

He left and dashed through the restaurant to the back.

Perk looked at Pearl, Ray, and Dutch. It was weird to not have Adam there, for even just a few moments. They all stared back at him as if he knew what to do. "Uh, so, yeah. Any ideas?"

Pearl set down her fork. "Well, we aren't going to do anything to hurt Mr. Parmar's car, right? We'll totally get caught and we'd get in so much trouble."

Perk cleared his throat and rubbed his hands on his jeans. "Yeah. I mean, no, that's definitely a rule. We can't damage anything. We can't stoop low like they do."

Adam dashed back through the restaurant and sat back down in his seat. He opened his computer and booted it up. "Anything yet?"

"Not yet," Perk said. "Just talking about how we can't ruin Parmar's car."

"True. I sort of wish that we could, though." Adam stared at his computer screen, pressing buttons.

"Maybe," Dutch said, squinting. "Maybe we can send Hill to a different camp?"

"That's a good idea," Pearl said. "What camp, though?"

"A really boring camp," Ray said. "Or . . . or a camp on something he doesn't know about. Like gymnastics camp or skateboarding camp. Is there a camp for bullies?"

"But won't his dad just get him out of it?" Perk asked.

"True," Pearl said.

"Then I guess we have to make sure he doesn't get into Camp Beaumont, or whatever it's called."

"How about a military boot camp?" Ray said. "My brother almost had to go to one a few years ago."

"But again, Mr. Parmar can get him out of it."

"We'll just have to make sure that he doesn't know that he's in a different camp until the bus takes him away," Ray said.

"That's good," Pearl said.

Perk was impressed. He hadn't expected good ideas from anyone except him and Adam.

"Yeah," Dutch continued. "We can send in a different video of him and then Mr. Parmar couldn't say anything."

"You mean, one of him bullying someone?"

Dutch shrugged.

"That's good," Perk said.

That's when Adam sat up straight and said, "Yes! I've got it."

CHAPTER 35

Ray

Ray had just plunged his spoon into the large, melty apple pie slice when Adam yelled. Ray's arm jerked, and he'd sent a glob of whipped cream soaring onto Dutch's plate.

"Oh man," he said. His face was heating up. "I'm sorry."

But Dutch laughed.

"Listen, guys," Adam said. He turned his computer around. "Look at this."

It was an old black-and-white photo. It was a photo of an old car—an Austin Seven, the article said—perched on top of a roof.

They were all crowded around the computer and

Adam leaned forward, tapping his finger on the screen. "This is what we need to do to Parmar's car."

Pearl laughed. "Really?"

"Sure. Look." He scrolled down the article. "They even have how they did it. It's genius."

"Yes," Dutch said. "I say let's do it."

Perk nodded. "We'll have to make sure we can get the materials, but I'm in." He laughed. "Can you imagine his face when he sees it."

"Can I look at the article?" Ray asked. He couldn't even guess how the car got on the roof.

Adam pushed it toward him. "Sure."

Everyone continued talking about the car on the roof while Ray examined the diagram and read the article. The maneuvering, the hoisting, the pulling, the scaffolding, steel wire rope. Three teams. The car was empty and inside the car they'd placed a pulley system for the steel wire rope to wrap around.

It was genius.

But there was no way they could do it without damaging the car. The school roof was lower than the roof in the picture, so they could possibly use a ramp or a lift . . . but still.

"So, what do you think, Ray?" Adam asked. "I know you're smarter than you let on." He turned to everyone. "Seriously, guys. I saw him take apart a calculator and put it back together, fixed, in science class one day. It was awesome."

"Well, it's really not that hard."

"Whatever," Adam said. "And today you didn't use your dad's lock cutter, right?"

Ray shrugged. "I know how to pick locks."

Adam laughed and leaned back. "This is gold. So come on, what do you think of the car on the roof?"

Heat filled Ray's face. "The idea is really cool, but—"

He paused. The feeling of being called smart, out loud, by someone surprised him in a good way. A really good way. And when he looked up at everyone, none of them seemed to be surprised at what Adam had said.

Could he tell them right now that he wasn't sure it was possible? They all thought he was smart. Maybe he could make it work.

"So, what do you think?" Adam asked again. Ray could tell he was excited.

Ray handed Adam his computer back. "I think it's an awesome idea," he said. "We'll figure it out."

CHAPTER 36
Pearl

She looked up from her cinnamon roll.

Ray didn't look very sure about the prank. But he also didn't look like he was as smart as Adam said he was. Then again, most people were surprised when they found out she was a violinist, as if she didn't look like one.

But what did a violinist look like?

What did a smart person look like?

Maybe no one was as they seemed or looked.

"So," Perk said. He dug his fork into the last bite of his cake. "Now that we know Ray is smart—"

"I never said—" Ray cut in.

Perk held up his hand. "Now that we know he's

smart, is there anything else that you guys can do or that you're good at? Something that could help us with the car or the camp?"

Pearl licked the icing off her fork. "I'm good at remembering things."

"Remembering?" Adam asked. "What do you mean?"

She could remember the music variation to all of her pieces from her first recital, the Latin roots for all the words they'd learned that year in English, the quadratic equation, the definition of direct, indirect, and controlled variables in science, and locker combinations. Her dad said she was sort of like Sherlock Holmes—bits of information were stored in places where she could access them if she just concentrated.

Everyone was looking at her.

"Do you have a photographic memory?" Dutch asked.

Pearl shook her head. "No. I forget things like anyone else. It's just that when I really want to remember something—numbers, music for a song, and facts are the easiest—I just . . . remember."

Adam's eyebrows lifted. "Really?"

She shrugged and tried not to smile at everyone looking at her. "Yeah. Stop looking at me like that."

Perk leaned forward. "Twenty-seven, forty-nine degrees latitude, three hundred fifty-two, sheep, book, aardvark, blue, window, rope. Say it backward, too."

Pearl sat up straighter, closed her eyes, and then rattled off everything that Perk had just said forward and backward. They all clapped. She pretended to bow. She'd had people clap for her before, but this felt different.

"Well, that will definitely come in handy," Adam said. "So, Dutch, how about you? You're probably a rocket scientist or something?"

Pearl glanced at Dutch, who smile-squinted and shook his head. "Nope. Nothing like that."

His smile reminded her of J. S. Bach's "Partita No. 3"—light and full and tripping on itself.

She closed her eyes a moment and hid his smile away in her head.

CHAPTER 37
Dutch

The lava cake made him feel warm and cozy inside, or maybe it was sitting so close to Pearl, he wasn't sure.

He'd just have to get used to that feeling.

Adam's question, "So, Dutch, how about you?" still hung in the air.

He shrugged. "I don't know. Nothing like you guys."

"It doesn't matter," Pearl said. "Come on. What are some things?"

If only he could say something like, I'm really good at rock climbing, or soccer, or he was an amazing writer, or he could sing really well. But there was nothing like that. "I can play cards and do some card tricks. And well, my grandpa says I can imitate people pretty good."

"Really?" Perk said. "That's cool."

He shrugged.

"Who can you imitate?" Adam asked.

"I don't know. It's not like any one person. Just people's voices I hear."

"Like Parmar's?"

Dutch knew where this was going. "Maybe."

Adam leaned forward and smiled. "Try."

Dutch glanced at Pearl.

"All right." He looked down and rubbed his face in an attempt to keep himself from smiling. He had to do a good job for Pearl.

"Well," he started, his voice low and catching the tiny inflections in Mr. Parmar's voice. "I'm sorry Hill locked you in the bathroom again. Boys will be boys. Just don't take it so seriously, son."

Everyone fell silent, staring at him. Adam knocked Perk with his elbow and they started laughing. "That was perfect!" Adam said.

"Creepy and awesome," Ray said. He was smiling.

Perk shook his head like he must have heard wrong. "I can't believe that."

"That sounded exactly like him," Pearl said. "Seriously, that was crazy. How did you do that?"

Dutch squinted. "I don't know." He squinted again. "My grandpa said my dad was good at imitating people, so maybe I inherited it or something. I've also had enough experience with Parmar telling me to 'take it like a man' and 'boys just being boys' and 'don't take it so seriously.'"

Their waitress walked over then, and Adam handed her his mostly clean plate. "Thanks, Mary," he said, and then to Dutch, "That is definitely going to come in handy at some point. These pranks are going to be awesome."

Dutch's chest and heart filled up like a helium balloon and floated around inside him.

It stayed with him as they all got up to go and thanked Adam's mom and dad and kept him buoyant even as he watched everyone leave one by one while he waited and waited and waited for his grandpa to come and get him.

"Hey, Dutch," Adam said, opening the door to

Bakers' Place. "My mom is dropping me off at home. She could take you if you want?"

The floating feeling sank a little inside him as he looked one more time down the empty street. "Yeah, that would be great. My grandpa might have fallen asleep or something." That could have been the case. Or he might have forgotten.

The floating, hopeful feeling had pretty much vanished by the time he thanked Adam's mom and walked up the stairs to the apartment. But then there was Gramps. He greeted Dutch with a smile and told him he'd missed him and asked if he wanted to play a game of cards before they "hit the hay."

"Sure," Dutch said, pulling up a chair and sitting down.

"Did you have a fun time with your friends?" he asked.

Dutch nodded. At least Gramps remembered some of the phone call from after school. "Yep, it was a lot of fun. They think I'm good at imitating people."

His grandpa dealt out the cards. "Of course you are." He looked at him with the mischievous grin he always got when they played cards. "But can you outwit an old fox like me?"

Dutch gave him the same look back. "I'm gonna try."

CHAPTER 38
Adam

The next afternoon, after school, Adam sat on his bed, re-rereading the article on the prank that he'd pulled up on his computer. He should leave for Perk's soon, right now really.

He read it one more time, wishing the description and the diagram would change.

Pulleys? Gutting the car? Steel rope? Three groups of five or eight people? Scaffolding?

He sighed.

There was no way.

Last night at the restaurant he'd been so starry-eyed with how their prank with Hill had turned out earlier in the day, and everyone's hidden talent, that he'd seen the picture of the car on the rooftop and knew that that was what they needed to do.

He hadn't even looked at the article. He'd seen the picture and diagram and that was all. It was big enough to get back at Hill and Parmar, big enough for Tommy.

He typed into his search bar "car pranks" and hit Enter.

Fill a car with marshmallows. Cover it with sticky notes. Park it somewhere else.

No, no, and definitely no.

Nothing would be good enough unless it was Parmar's Shelby Cobra on top of the school roof.

There was another article about a car on a roof. They'd got it up there using ramps.

Adam leaned back and closed his laptop. He wasn't quite sure how that would work, but still, it proved that they could do it a different way. And Ray had looked at the article last night. "We'll figure it out." That's what Ray had said.

And they had Dutch and Pearl, too.

"Yeah, we'll figure it out," Adam said aloud.

He gathered up a thick pad of paper, the calendars

he'd written up for Perk to look at, and his laptop, then stuffed them into his backpack along with clean underwear for the morning. The only thing he needed now were pencils. Perk should have them, but for some reason his family seemed to have things like exotic cheese, two hot tubs, eight bedrooms, and a personalized embossing stamp for books, but they didn't have things like pencils, Post-it notes, or milk.

He walked into the kitchen where his mom and dad were already fixing dinner. Both of them were wearing—as they did almost every Friday night—their Mr. and Mrs. aprons they had bought each other for Christmas last year. By the smell of it, they were making something with crab.

The perfect meal to disappear for.

Adam hated crab.

"You heading over to Perk's now?" his dad asked, sprinkling salt into a pot of boiling water.

Adam smiled and rifled through the junk drawer. "Yeah. We're going to work on a project for school."

"Oh yeah," his mom said. "Is everyone in the group going?"

"I don't know." As far as he knew right now, it was

just him, Perk, and Tommy.

"Should I invite everyone over?" Perk had asked after lunch. "What do you think?"

Adam had nodded. "Sure. We can start planning now that we know what we want to do. And Tommy would love having everyone over, I'm sure."

"Yeah," Perk said, and smiled. "He would, wouldn't he? I'll think about it."

But Perk rarely did anything without overthinking it. Adam could practically picture him racking his brain over the idea right then.

"They all seem like good kids," Adam's mom said. "And it sure looked like you all were having a great time the other night."

Adam grabbed a few pencils and stuffed them into his backpack. "Yeah, it was a lot of fun." And it had been.

"Are you guys getting work done, too?" Adam's mom pulled down a plastic container and filled it with cookies.

Adam slung the backpack over his shoulder and took the container. "A little of both."

CHAPTER 39
Perk

Perk had a lot of good ideas. Like mixing M&M's in popcorn, or arranging his and Adam's school schedule, or buying three of Tommy's favorite shirts so that he could alternate them in the wash.

But asking Ray, Pearl, and Dutch over to his house with Adam to talk about the prank—well, he wasn't so sure.

That's why he hadn't.

Yet.

"Your turn, Perk," Tommy said. He handed Perk the dice and Perk rolled and moved and paid Tommy for landing on his property, though he didn't really know how much because he wasn't paying much attention to the game.

On one hand, it would be nice to hang out with just Adam and Tommy and play games and goof around like they always did. Easy. Predictable. But he'd had so much fun with everyone the other night, and they were all friends now so he didn't have to be nervous about anything, and really they needed to work on the details of the prank.

"Your turn again, Perk."

Perk rolled the dice and then Tommy laughed and jumped up and danced around like he did every time Perk didn't realize that Tommy had landed on his property. "That's what you get for not paying attention, Perk. You always have to pay attention. Always."

Perk nodded and smiled. "Yeah, that was my fault."

He could still ask them. After all, he had all of their phone numbers and e-mails . . . and a whole lot of other things, too, like their schedules, grades, and extracurricular activities, but that was beside the point. He hadn't called anyone besides Adam, his parents, Tommy's school, and the pizza guy in . . . well, ever.

"Can we have special popcorn, Perk, with M&M's? Adam likes them, too, and Adam is coming over, and you said we could have special popcorn because I missed going to the restaurant. You promised."

"Yeah, sure." Perk got up, opened a bag of popcorn, and took down the bag of candy he kept hidden behind the container of organic granola.

He tried to picture the group standing in the foyer, looking around with that openmouthed gape that most people got when they walked inside.

He hated that face. And actually, besides the occasional trip to somewhere exotic, or enough spending money that he could buy any candy he wanted, Perk hated being rich. He'd much rather get by all right like Adam's parents.

The microwave beeped and Perk pulled out the bag of popcorn and dumped it into the green popcorn bowl. His stomach rumbled and he reached into the small jar of spending money that stood beside the Shabbat candles. There was a wad of bills and a note scratched on the back of a magazine: "*Get yourself and Tommy some pizza tonight. Remind Tommy to not blow out the candles; he forgets sometimes. We'll be home late. Love you, Rachel*" but the name *Rachel* had been scratched out and *Mom* was written next to it.

She signed her name a lot so it had happened before. He didn't mind.

"You hungry?" Perk asked. "We could order pizza?"

"Yes!" Tommy said, pumping his fist into the air. "I love pizza."

Perk dialed the number.

"Pizza Plaza. What can I get for you?"

Perk hesitated. Four pizzas would be enough for him and everyone else.

He felt like he was standing on the edge of the pool deciding whether to jump in or not.

"Hello? Anyone there?"

"Yeah, sorry," Perk said. "I'd like an order for delivery please."

"Great, what can I get you?"

He only needed two for himself and Tommy and Adam.

"Sir?"

Perk shrugged and then leaped off the edge.

"I'll take four pizzas. Two cheese, one veggie, and one barbeque chicken."

"Is that all?"

"Yep."

"We'll be there in thirty minutes or less."

Perk hung up and took a deep breath. He grabbed a big bill from the money jar and stuffed it into his pocket.

"Is all that pizza for us?" Tommy asked.

Perk tossed the empty bag of popcorn into the trash and pulled out three more bags of popcorn. "Actually, we're going to have a few more people come over."

He glanced around, his eyes falling on his notes about alarm systems and the blueprints of the school he had managed to get. He'd show everyone what he had worked on so far. He grabbed the info folder he'd created.

"Oh good. I'm going to invite everyone to my art show," Tommy said. "Especially Pearl. Can I?"

Perk nodded at his brother, then picked up the phone again and dialed the first number on the list.

"Yeah, can I speak to Ray, please?"

CHAPTER 40
Ray

Ray's shoes scuffled on the sidewalk, opening up the small hole at the toe a little more.

Fifteen minutes ago he'd put on his shoes and tugged on his sweatshirt. "I'm going to a friend's house," he'd called.

Silence.

He opened the door just wide enough to squeeze himself out, but small enough to keep the stray cat that he'd given a saucer of milk to, from slipping inside.

"I'll be back later on tonight," he yelled again, this time through the screen.

Not like they would've noticed or cared either way.

His brother, dad, and pappy were already sitting

down, pizza steaming in their laps, waiting for the fight to start. They had their bets on the table, and Ray was sure that a couple of guys from the shop would be coming over soon. With everyone piled around the television, there wouldn't be much room for him anyway.

So when Perk called, he'd said sure, memorized the directions to his house, and grabbed his unused notebook, stuffing it into his backpack.

He still didn't know how he was going to make Adam's idea work. There was too much risk of the car getting dented, scratched, or worse, not to mention getting scaffolding, steel rope, and rigging an entire pulley system.

He'd looked up other ways to get a car up on a roof at the school library earlier and saw that one group of kids had used a series of ramps to drive the car onto the roof. That would be perfect, except for the minor detail of finding ramps, getting them to the school, and then taking them away.

The only other thing that might work were the lifts at his dad's garage. Maybe. It depended on the width of the car and the height of the school, not to mention keeping it from his dad.

On his way to Perk's, the houses seemed to grow taller and wider, the lawns more well-groomed, and the gates higher. 252 Bradbury Court. It even sounded rich. Ray felt the urge to duck his head, smooth out his shirt, and make himself look smaller—less noticeable. That, however, was pretty much impossible.

But the other night when he was sitting at Bakers' Place with everyone, laughing, he'd felt normal, like an average kid hanging out with his friends on a Thursday night.

Then again, he was sitting down for most of the time, so maybe that was why he felt normal. It was easier to make himself look smaller when he sat down.

He turned down the road just as a car pulled up alongside him. Probably a cop. This had happened to him before—cops stopping him and asking him what he thought he was doing. He knew he wasn't teddy-bear friendly looking or a big-fat-rich-kid, so he should've expected he'd get stopped.

The car slowed and he picked up his pace, his breath coming faster. 252 Bradbury Court. He only had a few more houses to go, and his dad would lose it if a cop escorted him home.

"Hey!"

Ray sped up his walk to a slow jog.

"Hey, Ray! It's me. Ray?!"

Ray turned around and saw Dutch squinting out the passenger-side window. He slowed down and stopped. "Oh hey. Sorry, I . . . I didn't know who it was."

"Better safe than sorry."

That wasn't what Ray meant, but that was okay.

The old man in the driver's seat leaned over and said something to him. Ray turned and continued down the sidewalk. He'd see Dutch in a minute or two.

"Hey, Ray."

"Yeah?"

"Want a ride the rest of the way? I know it's not far, but still."

Ray looked down the sidewalk.

"Come on, Ray," the old man called out. "We don't bite. Promise."

Ray let a small smile cross his lips and hopped in. "Thanks."

Well, he definitely didn't feel normal or average right now, sitting in Dutch's mini car. His head grazed the top of the old car, and his knees smashed against the worn front seat.

"I'm Dutch's grandpa. Dutch tells me you're one of the brains behind the school project?" the old man said.

Brains? Really? Ray felt his cheeks burn. "Uh . . . I don't know."

Dutch turned around and squinted a smile. "Of course you are, Ray."

The car squeaked to a stop and Dutch's grandfather looked at the number on the gate. "Who-weee. That's a palace if I've ever seen one." He knocked Dutch with his elbow.

"Yeah."

Ray opened the car door and spilled out. "Thank you, sir," he said.

"My pleasure. I can take you home, too, if you'd like? I'm picking up Dutch around nine-thirty or so. Can't stay up too much past my bedtime." He smiled and winked.

"Sure, thanks."

"Thanks," Dutch said.

When the car pulled away from the curb, Dutch

and Ray started up the drive to the gate.

"I bet you already have some ideas on how to engineer everything."

Ray shrugged. "Some."

"Are you going to show us?"

"Sure."

They pressed an intercom button, and then Perk and Tommy's face appeared on the TV monitor and the gate buzzed open.

Dutch and Ray looked at each other.

For the second time that day, Ray didn't feel gigantic and he didn't feel small.

He felt like an average, normal kid about to hang out with his friends on a Friday night.

He could get used to it.

CHAPTER 41
Pearl

The houses blurred past as Pearl's mom drove down the road, speaking the directions out loud every time they came to another intersection. She always did that when she drove.

"Left on Bradbury, go about a half mile, fourth house on the right."

Perk's call couldn't've come at a better time.

Her dad had just gotten home from another business trip that morning, and he'd taken her out of school for lunch. They'd gone to a little deli, and Pearl hadn't been able to keep her excitement down when he started to talk about how much he had missed her and her mom on this trip. He had made dinner reservations for the three of them at a restaurant, but Pearl wanted them to be alone with each other.

Out on a date.

So when Perk called, Pearl told her mom and dad that she had to go—it was an urgent meeting for their group project. This was, of course, true, though minus the word "urgent." But in a way, even that was true.

It was urgent for her parents to be together.

"What are you and Dad going to do? You know, while I'm gone?"

Her mother leaned forward and looked at the road name. "McKenzie Lane. That should take us there." She turned the car and they started down the street lined with huge houses. She shrugged. "Oh, I don't know. Your father said that we should keep the dinner reservation, so I think we'll do that."

Pearl smiled and glanced out the window. "That'll be fun."

Her hopeful song, "Spiegel im Spiegel," played through her head as the fingers on her left hand fluttered out the notes.

"Did you end up playing for the special education class at the high school today?" her mom asked, followed by a mumbled, "Bradbury should be down here somewhere."

"Yeah, we went right at the end of school and played a few songs. Perk's brother goes there, so I got to see him."

"Really? That's nice. Anyone else I know that was there?"

"Callie, Stu, Joanna, Sari, Hill, and a few others."

"Bradbury. Here it is." She turned the car and leaned forward, trying to see the house numbers. "Hill. He was a nice boy, wasn't he? I didn't know he played an instrument."

Pearl cringed. "He doesn't. He was there to get volunteer hours and he didn't do anything except sit back in this old recliner, order a few of the kids around, and then drink a few juice boxes that were meant for the students. So no, he's not nice. But he's good at fooling people."

"That's unfortunate."

Watching Hill in Tommy's classroom made her sick. He cringed when one of the kids tried to hold his hand and when Hill pulled his hand away, he immediately washed it in the sink. At the end, he'd pushed through the front doors and said, "Seriously, that was just gross.

I'm gonna kill my dad for making me do that."

Pearl's mom stopped the car and leaned over Pearl to see the number on the gate. "Two fifty-two. This is beautiful."

Pearl reached into the backseat for her backpack, then opened the car door.

"So what time should I pick you up?" her mom asked.

She stepped onto the sidewalk and pulled her backpack straps over her shoulders. "Oh, I don't know. I don't want to interrupt your and dad's night."

"It's all right. You won't be."

"No really, I bet that Dutch and his grandpa could give me a ride home."

Her mom shrugged. "Well, call me and let me know. Either way, I want you home by nine-thirty."

"Okay." She started up to the gate. "Thanks, Mom. Have fun."

As the car pulled away, Pearl stepped up to the intercom and pressed the button. Tommy's face appeared on the screen. "Hello, do we know you?"

Pearl smiled and waved into the camera. "Hi, Tommy. It's me, Pearl."

"Okay." He turned his head off to the side. "Perk, it's the pretty girl. She's here!" He turned back to her. "Hi, Pearl."

Her cheeks reddened. "Hi, Tommy."

"Do you remember when I told you about my art show today at school?" he asked. "Can you come? Please? Everyone is going to come. I invited Adam and Perk and Ray and Dutch and my mom and my dad and my—"

"All right, Tommy," Perk cut in. "Let her in and you can tell her all about it."

"Okay. But will you come?"

"Of course I'll come," she said, and then stepped through the gate when it buzzed.

"Hi," Tommy said, opening up the door just as she reached the porch. "You look the same as you did at my school. We have pizza. Do you like pizza?"

"I do." Inside, she instantly caught sight of Dutch. Her happy song, "Hobo's Blues," trilled through her when he smile-squinted at her. She smiled back and everything sort of blurred just for a triple-time-moment.

She wasn't expecting that.

CHAPTER 42

Dutch

1. Go to Perk's house
2. Gramps would pick him up in a few hours

There was a wrestling match going on inside him.

He and his grandpa spent almost every single evening together.

No, that wasn't right.

It wasn't *almost*, it was *always*—Every. Single. Night.

They would play cards, or they would read together. Gramps would tell him old stories, or they'd watch old movies. And because Dutch wasn't there tonight, Grandpa would be alone. Dutch could practically see him sitting at the small table, maybe playing solitaire, eating grilled cheese (would he remember to turn off the stove?), wishing that Dutch was there, and always wishing that Grammie was there.

Sometimes it seemed like he really thought that she was just out at the store, or reading in the bedroom, or taking a walk down the block to where there was a small forest area.

Those were the times that Dutch worried most.

He did feel a little better, though. He'd looked online at a discussion board for people who have family members who were losing their memories. Dutch couldn't call it dementia and he wouldn't call it Alzheimer's, but after Gramps had woken up the night before calling for Grammie from his bed, he'd decided to look a little more at the discussion boards.

Dutch hadn't posted anything, but he read a little. And then Gramps seemed fine all day, encouraging him to go out with his friends. It was different every day. Every moment, almost.

"I'll be fine," he'd said, ruffling Dutch's hair. "It'll be good for you and that means that it'll be good for me, too."

Now, Dutch felt guilty for having fun. For being with his friends—and he'd never been able to say the word "friend," let alone "friends" before. But they'd laughed at his jokes and didn't seem to notice that he squinted whenever his face felt like squinting.

He wanted to be with his grandpa.

But he wanted to be here . . . more.

Was that bad?

And of course there was Pearl.

Pearl was there. She was smiling and happy and didn't have that faraway look in her eyes like she did the time at Adam's house.

And she'd touched his arm. Just really quick. But she did.

And she blushed. He knew it was ridiculous to think that she blushed because of him. But she had blushed.

He was sure of it.

"Do that one trick with the three piles of cards that you showed us before Pearl came," Adam said, interrupting Dutch's thoughts. "That's your best one."

They were all sitting in Perk's massive living room. Or was this the game room, or the lounge, or the courtyard? Whatever it was, it was a really big room. He and Gramps's entire apartment was about this size.

Ray shrugged and grinned, going through the trick again.

Dutch's grandpa had taught him a few card tricks when he was little. They were pretty good, though he wasn't sure if his hand would be steady enough.

He watched Pearl smile and point to a pile of cards and wish that he remembered.

Adam laughed at the end, when his card—the seven of spades—appeared. "That is so cool."

Dutch had no idea how Ray did it.

"Come on," Pearl said. "You have to tell me how you did that."

Her cheeks were pink and Dutch had to look away. Was she blushing now because of Ray? Being back at their small apartment with Gramps, suddenly felt like a good place to be. "Just a little sleight of hand," Ray said. "The trick is to get the person focused on something other than what you're trying to do."

That was right.

When Dutch wasn't looking, Ray pulled a sleight of hand with Pearl.

But no. Dutch shook his head, hoping to get the sense back inside. Pearl wasn't like that. She was nice to him, just like she had always been nice to everyone. She didn't like Dutch, but she also didn't like Ray, and that made him feel a little better, though he wasn't sure if it should.

Dutch took another slice of pizza and sat on the floor.

"Okay," Pearl said. She smiled and sat down in front of him, her plate of pizza on her lap. "Now I have a card trick I'm going to try on you, Dutch," she said. "My aunt taught it to me a while ago so hopefully I remember."

He wished she wasn't so kind and her smile wasn't so wide.

"You ready?"

He nodded. He might just ask her to do the trick over and over and over again . . . just to keep her sitting and smiling in front of him.

CHAPTER 43
Adam

"You can't move a piece like that, Adam," Tommy said. He laughed. "The horse can only do this or that. Okay?"

"Got it." Adam moved the horse in the direction that Tommy had instructed and sighed. He hadn't played chess since he was seven. Tommy had asked him to play before, but Adam had always been able to distract him. But tonight Tommy had been so anxious to play chess with Ray, saying, "When's he coming?" "Do you think he'll play with me?" "I can't wait to play chess with Ray" that Adam found himself volunteering to start a game before Ray even came.

He and Tommy were like brothers and that's what brothers did.

Now he wished he was sitting in the living room with everyone else. He hadn't liked playing chess back then and even less now. Sitting, staring, and waiting was not his thing. Plotting and then getting things done was more his style. "So, Tommy," he said, taking a bite of his pizza. "What would you think if you saw a car on a roof?"

Tommy looked up from the board. "Why would there be a car on a roof? Like Wacky Wednesday?"

Adam nodded and moved his knight back to where it was before. He'd like to just quit, but Tommy hated to quit games. If he remembered more about the game, maybe he could lose on purpose? "Yeah, like Wacky Wednesday. Would you think that was a good trick?"

Tommy laughed. "Yes. That would be so funny."

Good. Tommy didn't know why they were going to do it, but it was important that he liked it.

"How would the car get there? Is it like magic?" Tommy asked. "It's your turn."

Adam looked over at Ray, who was sitting in the living room, a plate on his lap. Had he figured out how to make the car on the roof work? "I don't know how it would get up there," Adam said as he moved his horse again. "But something else would be really funny, too, right? Fill a car with marshmallows or something?" It still sounded silly but just in case.

"I'd like to eat marshmallows." Tommy swiped his nose.

"How about seeing them in a car? A whole car filled with marshmallows."

Tommy paused and tapped his chin. "I like the car on the roof. And then I'd want to eat all the marshmallows."

"Yeah, me, too."

Tommy sighed and looked at the chessboard. "You're not very good, Adam."

Adam laughed. "I know, right?"

"Can I play with Ray? I don't want to hurt your feelings 'cause that isn't nice, but you're not very good."

He wasn't hurt. "Sure. Hey, Ray," he called into the living room. "I think Tommy wants a more worthy opponent."

"Yeah, a worthy opponent," Tommy repeated.

"Sure." Ray carried his plate over to the kitchen table and took Adam's spot. Not his spot in Tommy's life, of course. That wouldn't happen.

Adam shifted to the chair in between, not quite ready to go into the living room yet. "So Tommy said that he'd like to see a car on a roof, too, but we can't figure out how someone could get it up there."

"Unless it was magic," Tommy said. He rearranged the pieces into their starting positions on the board.

Ray shrugged. "Well, it depends on the car. They definitely can't use the steel ropes and cables 'cause it'll ruin the car."

"Ramps?" Adam asked.

"Maybe, but I just don't know how they'd get them."

"Then what?"

"I don't know. Lifts, maybe, but I'm not sure if the car's wide enough or the lifts could go high enough."

Tommy took one of Ray's pawns. "Are you gonna put a car on a roof? I saw a giant snowman on a roof before."

"That's cool," Ray said.

Adam stood up, trying to ignore the annoying worry that was trying to climb to the surface. "Nothing can top a prank like that. You're smart enough to figure out a way, right?"

Ray squirmed a little in his seat. "Sure." He moved his rook. "Your move, Tommy."

CHAPTER 44
Perk

The pizza boxes were now empty but for a few lone pepperonis and tossed-aside crusts.

Perk looked over at the kitchen. His best friend had abandoned the chess game—he was surprised Adam had lasted as long as he had—but it looked like Ray and Tommy had just begun playing. If he didn't stop it before too long, there would be no distracting Tommy.

"Hey, guys," he said. He grabbed a piece of discarded crust and took a bite. "Let's get started."

"But we did just start, Perk. We need to finish our game," Tommy said.

"Sorry, but they can't stay for too much longer, and

we need to talk about stuff all together, okay? You can sit over here with us."

Tommy leaned back in his chair and folded his arms across his chest. "Why can't Ray and I listen and play chess at the same time? Sometimes you do that, Perk."

"I hardly ever do that," Perk said. "But come on. You can come in here and talk with us." Perk started putting the pieces away, silently praying Tommy wouldn't throw one of his fits.

"We'll play next time," Ray said. "Come on. You can sit by me." Ray started for the living room, and Tommy stood up and plopped down next to him.

Disaster averted. He owed Ray.

"So," Adam was saying, "Ray is taking care of the car thing. Now we need to plan out what we're going to do with the prestigious Camp Beaumont that Hill is hoping to go to this summer."

"Hey, Perk," Tommy said. "Tell them about the camp that I'm going to this summer. Tell them."

Perk turned to Tommy. "Not now, maybe in a bit, okay?"

"It's going to be the best camp in the world. I've

never been but that's what the man said. He said, 'The best camp in the world.'"

"Yep, he did, Tommy. Now you need to be quiet so we can talk about something really important, okay?"

"Okay." He pretended to zip up his lips, lock them, and then toss away the key.

Perk began again. "Camp Beaumont says that they need a video of Hill. Ray overheard Parmar say that they hadn't made the video yet—"

"I think it's done now," Pearl interjected. "Hill was talking about it at lunch today."

"Really?" Perk reached for his computer and opened it. "That means we've gotta move fast. I just hope he hasn't e-mailed it off yet." Perk logged onto Parmar's e-mail and checked his Sent messages. Whew. "Looks like we lucked out." He checked Parmar's desktop and downloads for a video. "It's here, but he hasn't done anything with it yet."

"But what if he sends it tomorrow, or in a few minutes, even?"

Perk clicked on the e-mail settings. "I'm going to change his e-mail password for now so he can't get in and I'll mess with his Wi-Fi. It'll hold him off for a little while, but I'll have to stay on it. On Monday we'll have to get a new video."

"What's the video of?" Tommy asked. "Can we watch it?"

Perk tried to ignore Tommy and continued on. "We need you for this part, Dutch."

"Me? Why me?"

"Perk?" Tommy asked again and tapped Perk on the shoulder. He shrugged it off. Perk hated to ask it of Dutch—Dutch got bullied enough as it was that asking him to purposefully set himself up to be picked on seemed cruel. "Well, we need to catch him in the act."

Dutch was quiet a moment and then Perk could tell he understood. "Oh."

"Yeah."

Tommy tapped Perk on the shoulder again and then pulled at his T-shirt sleeve. "Perk. I have an e-mail now. People can e-mail me if they want."

"You're right," Perk said quickly. "I'll give it to everyone before they leave."

"There has to be another way to catch him at it," Pearl said.

Dutch shrugged. "But not another way to guarantee

we get a video. I get it." He paused. "I said I was in from the beginning so . . . I'm in."

Ray reached over and patted Dutch on the shoulder. "I'll make sure to be nearby."

"Perk?" Tommy said.

Perk shh'ed him.

"Perk," Tommy half whispered.

Perk stood up. "Sorry, guys," he said. "You keep talking. I'm just going to get Tommy busy with something else." He pulled his brother to his feet.

"But I don't want to do anything else. I want to be here."

Perk led him out of the room as he continued to protest. It was times like these that it would just be better if Tommy wasn't so . . . so Tommy. "I know," Perk said. He breathed deep and popped in *Finding Nemo*. He'd only lost his temper once with Tommy and he wasn't about to let it happen again. "Do you want to watch *Finding Nemo*?"

Tommy looked at him as if Perk was trying to trick him into eating mashed potatoes—Tommy's least favorite food. "But I want to see everyone."

Perk pushed Play and Tommy instinctively grabbed

his beanbag chair. "You will. I'll make sure they say good-bye, and Adam is spending the night, so you'll get to see him."

Music began behind him and Tommy brought his finger to his mouth. "Shh, Perk. It's starting."

Perk sighed and rubbed his brother's hair and then went out to rejoin the group.

Adam had already given the old iPod to Ray, who was busy taking it apart while Pearl ran through everything out loud.

"So I put the bug in Hill's ear about Dutch's iPod, which doesn't work, and the science paper. You and Perk set up one of those mini video cameras on top of the trophy case across from Dutch's locker. Hill comes by, bullies Dutch, and steals the iPod because he thinks it works; Ray stops him before it gets bad. Then we switch out the videos?" She paused. "How are we going to do that?"

Adam looked over for Perk to answer. "I don't have computer class on Monday and my parents will kill me if I bring mine to school, so I'll have to get on his computer, upload our video, and delete his. Does that work for everyone?"

They all nodded.

Around nine-thirty Pearl, Ray, and Dutch left, Dutch's grandpa driving everyone home.

Perk closed the front door, then started cleaning up the kitchen with Adam. "I think this is all going to work, don't you?" They seemed to have the plan for Hill really nailed down now. Getting the video would be easy, and then they just had to wait.

"Yeah, now Ray just has to figure out the car on the roof." Adam stacked a plate in the dishwasher.

"Maybe we should come up with another plan for the car?" Even as Perk was saying it, Adam was shaking his head. He should've known. It was impossible to change Adam's mind.

"No, nothing else is even close to being big enough."

The sooner they got the whole car thing figured out, the better.

CHAPTER 45
Ray

He didn't have much time.

"One hour," his dad said. He wiped a grease-covered hand along his pants. "I better see your butt back in this shop by two or you'll be pulling a double shift for the next month. Understand?"

"I'll be back." Ray ducked out the front door and started down the street. Two blocks to the library. He picked up his pace. Making it there with enough time wouldn't be hard; he just hoped that there was an open computer—not always easy to come by on a Saturday—and he was able to find the information he needed. But what worried him most was *not* finding what he hoped, what he needed, what Adam and

Tommy and everyone else needed.

Pushing through the doors, he swept a hand across the sweat on his forehead before finding the bathroom and washing his dirty hands. The two tables of computers were mostly open, and he quickly signed the sheet for a thirty-minute session.

"Hi, Ray."

Ray turned. "Hi, Mrs. Potter." The school counselor was nice, even if she tried a little too hard sometimes to be everyone's friend.

"What are you up to today?"

He shrugged. "Nothing much."

She scanned his shirt and pants, both smeared with grease and dirt, his orange wax towel hanging out of his pocket. "Were you at your dad's shop?"

"Yeah. Lunch break." Time was ticking.

She nodded. "I saw that you're planning on taking the automotive technology track in high school."

"Yeah."

Her hands were folded in front of her, holding on to her purse. "You're not interested in taking the regular diploma track?"

He shrugged. "I don't know."

"I think you'd do great."

He shrugged again.

"Well," Mrs. Potter said. "Let me know if you change your mind and I can help you work with your schedule."

He nodded.

"I won't keep you any longer. See you at school."

"Bye."

She walked off.

He should've said thanks. Maybe he should've said "Yeah, can you change my schedule?"

Either way, it didn't matter now. She was gone and he had things to look up.

After getting online he typed "length and width of Shelby Cobra" in the search bar and hit Enter.

His heart sank in his chest.

It wouldn't fit on the jack.

He sighed and leaned back in the chair, then clicked off the computer. Two jacks maybe? One half of the car on one jack and the other half of the car on the other? Then it was getting the jacks to the school and back to his dad's garage by morning.

If his dad found out . . . well, he pushed that thought away.

The clock above his head said one-twenty. He still had time, but he should probably head back. Ray stood, checked his name off the list, and then walked out into the Saturday sun.

The walk back to the shop dragged, but he pushed through the door in time.

"Where've you been?" his dad said. He tossed him another rag. "There's a car waiting for you in stall three. Go take care of it."

CHAPTER 46
Pearl

Monday. Pearl walked into the cafeteria with her lunch, sat down, and searched the buzzing room. Dutch walked by with a lunch tray and Ray sat in a corner pulling something out of a crumpled brown paper bag. Adam and Perk were hopefully busy setting up the little video camera across from Dutch's locker.

"Come on, Mrs. Bali. He tripped."

Pearl spotted Hill.

The lunch aide, Mrs. Bali, was talking to him, and Pearl could see Hill's hands lifting in a "what-did-I-do-it-was-an-accident" sort of way.

Whatever he had done, he'd get off the hook. He always did.

Unless.

She might not be an Adam Baker or a Perkins Irving, but maybe she could get back at Hill in some small way?

Pearl scanned the lunchroom and found Jordan McDonald sitting at the table near the front of the lunch line, his tray filled with spilled chocolate milk and his misshapen glasses beside him. That must've been what Hill had "accidentally" done. Dutch sat next to him.

"I'm going to get some pretzels," Pearl said. No one seemed to hear her, or at least no one said anything back, so she got up, left her sandwich, apples, and chips on the table and made her way to the lunch line.

But before taking a place behind Hill, Pearl walked up to Jordan. She chanced a glance at Dutch and he smiled. "Hey, Jordan," she said.

He looked up at her. "Uh . . . uh . . . hi?"

"I was wondering if I could borrow your lunch card for a minute. I'm not going to use it, promise."

He shook his head and looked down. "I don't think so."

Dutch leaned over to him. "No, it's okay. You can trust her," he said.

Jordan gave him a you-can't-be-serious look then sighed and slid the card over. "You'll give it back?"

"Of course. Oh, and Dutch, if you could let Mrs. Bali know that Hill took Jordan's lunch card, I'd appreciate it."

He grinned and squinted. "Sure."

Jordan asked something else, but Pearl was already making her way to the lunch line.

Here goes nothing.

She strolled over and "accidentally" bumped into Hill. "Oh, sorry, Hill."

He turned and grinned at her. "Hey, no worries, Pearl. You can bump into me anytime. Actually, how about dancing with me at the spring dance?"

Pearl ignored him. "So, hey, did you finish the essay for science yet? I'm not sure if I did it right."

He raised his eyebrows. "What essay?"

"That one on the different types of cells. It was confusing how she wanted us to do it. It took a lot longer than I thought it would."

"Uh, no," Hill said. "I . . . uh, haven't finished yet. When is it due?"

"Tomorrow." Pearl's stomach twisted out of tune

inside her as she continued. "Dutch showed me his, and it looks really good."

Hill looked over at Dutch. "Really?" Then he grabbed his lunch tray and turned back to her. "That's good to know."

She shrugged and smiled. "Well, see ya."

She grabbed a bag of pretzels, paid her fifty cents, and walked off, sitting down at the table ready to watch her little plan unfold.

Dutch walked up to Mrs. Bali, squinting as he told her.

Mrs. Bali nodded at him, then walked over to Pearl's table, her hands on her formidable hips.

"Hill Parmar," Mrs. Bali said, holding out her hand. "It seems you've taken someone's lunch card?"

"What are you talking about?" Hill asked. "No, I didn't."

"Don't try this with me again," the woman said. "Just empty your pockets."

He pulled out a stick of gum, a five-dollar bill, an eraser, and Jordan McDonald's lunch card. "But I don't know how this got here. Seriously."

"Come with me, young man."

Pearl watched Hill follow Mrs. Bali out of the lunchroom and to the office. It actually worked! Her fingers fluttered over imaginary strings. She'd done it. Sure, she'd still set Dutch up to be bullied by Hill, but at least she'd gotten him back for Jordan, too.

At the end of lunch, Pearl gathered up her things and started for class. "Hey, Pearl." She turned to see Dutch. "Thanks for that," he said. He squinted over and over again. "That was really cool."

Her cheeks were hot and her heart skipped a note or two. "I can't believe it worked."

Dutch shrugged. "I can."

They were both silent, the rush of students milling through the hall blurry in the background.

"Jordan and I made this for you. It's just out of a paper napkin." Dutch held out a white paper flower. "My grandpa taught me."

"Wow, thanks." Pearl twirled it around her fingers. "It's really cool."

He shrugged. "Well, I better get to class." Squint.

"Yeah, me, too." Could he see how red her cheeks were? She turned and walked to her locker, placing the flower on the top shelf where it wouldn't be crushed.

"Hey, Pearl," Sari said. She leaned on the locker next to Pearl's. "You ready to go to class?"

"Sure." Pearl closed her locker.

"What are you smiling at?" Sari asked.

Pearl shrugged. "Oh, nothing."

CHAPTER 47
Dutch

1. Stay near locker
2. Wait for Hill to walk by
3. Let him see iPod
4. Give him fake homework assignment
5. Pray he doesn't drag me to bathroom

Dutch was glad that Ray was nearby fiddling with something in his locker. He was prepared to get hauled off to the bathroom as always, but he was hoping that with Ray there he could avoid it.

Hill had followed him to his locker after lunch . . . waiting, circling, just like a shark.

Mrs. Bali had made him return the lunch card to Jordan, apologize, and then sentenced him to a week of eating lunch in the office.

"I'll get out of it," Dutch had heard him brag. "I always do."

"That was still really cool," Jordan had told Dutch. "I can't believe Pearl Wagoner did that."

"Yeah."

Pearl was a lot braver than Dutch had thought.

And had he—squinting, dorky Dutch really given her—the brave, smart, beyond-beautiful Pearl Wagoner—a paper rose?

His face squinted again and again at the thought.

Maybe he was braver than he thought?

Ray coughed loud into his hand and when Dutch looked up, he nodded.

Dutch took a breath in. His throat felt sticky and he had the feeling of plunging headlong on a roller coaster.

He opened his locker and pulled out the nonworking, disassembled-and-then-reassembled iPod and set it on the top shelf of his locker so Hill could see it. Hill was behind him now; he could feel it. Dutch was glad that Pearl wasn't nearby watching. He didn't want her to see him scared, humiliated, pushed around. Even if he had volunteered for it.

"Nice iPod, freak." Hill leaned against the locker next to Dutch's and sneered. "I'm surprised you can afford something like that. And actually, I'm not sure someone like you should have something so nice.

"Well," Hill continued. "I appreciate you giving it to me." He reached up and took it. "I already have one, but it's always nice to have another."

"Don't, please," Dutch said.

He laughed. "Pwetty pwease?" he said in a mock baby voice. "Sorry, freak." He held the iPod up and looked at it, then smiled and slipped it into his pocket. He leaned against the locker again. "Hey, I hear you have the science essay done."

"Science essay?"

"Yeah, stupid," Hill said. "Did you even learn to read?" He pushed Dutch against his locker just enough that the metal rattled against Dutch's shoulders. "Now give it to me. I need it."

"Okay, okay." When Hill backed away a little, Dutch opened his backpack and pulled out an essay copied straight from one of their textbooks.

Hill snatched it up and nodded. "Good job, Dutch

Dork." He laughed. "I'll make sure to get a really good grade on it." He pushed Dutch against the locker once more and turned to leave, immediately ramming into Ray's chest.

Ray squared his shoulders and Dutch watched his fists clench. "There a problem here, Dutch?" he asked.

Hill backed away a little and made to pass him. "Nothing, man. Dutch here was just helping me with some homework. Right, freak?"

At that, Ray slammed Hill into the locker. "His name is Dutch," he spat. Then he turned to Dutch. "You good?"

Dutch nodded and looked from one to the other.

Ray looked just as terrifying as Hill did—maybe even more. Bigger and broader, he loomed over Hill, his face inches from Hill's.

If someone didn't know better, they'd think that Ray was bullying Hill rather than defending a friend.

Hill sidestepped Ray and started down the hallway, turning once to sneer at Dutch.

"Was that enough for the video?" Dutch whispered.

Ray slapped Dutch on the back. "Oh yeah. We got him."

CHAPTER 48
Adam

Adam's mission? "Distract Ms. Gingko for Perk."

Perk's mission? "Get inside Parmar's office with the mini video camera, delete the real video, replace it with our video, and get out."

Ms. Gingko was peeling an orange when Adam walked in, claiming he needed to wait there for his mom to pick him up. "Dentist appointment," he said.

"I can call you down when she arrives," Ms. Gingko said.

"Can I just wait here for a few minutes?" Adam asked. "If she doesn't come by in a few, I'll go back to class." He used the face that usually worked well with most teachers.

Ms. Gingko sighed. "Five minutes, Mr. Baker."

Just then, the school nurse walked in. "Is Mr. Parmar here?"

"His meeting should be almost done," Ms. Gingko said. She brushed the orange peel into her small garbage can.

"Has his new desk arrived?"

"Yes, so he'll spend the rest of the day organizing, I'm sure. It's a mess right now."

Parmar's office was a mess and he got a new desk? Where was his computer?

Adam stood up. "Actually, Ms. Gingko," he said starting for the hall. "I think my appointment is for tomorrow. Sorry." He started off without waiting for her response.

What should he do? Think.

First: find Perk. Then . . . Dutch. Yes, that's who he needed.

He walked out of the office and started for Perk's third-period class—language arts. He had to get him before he walked into the office. He rounded a corner and almost ran into him. "Oh, hey."

"Why aren't you in the office?"

"Change of plans. Parmar had a new desk delivered so his office is a disaster. I'm assuming his computer's still there, but I'm not sure."

"Shoot." He shrugged. "Well, we've gotta try. He could send off Hill's application any second."

"All right," Adam said. "You stay in the bathroom and then in five minutes head to the office. I have an idea."

He rifled through his brain at the lists of schedules he'd tried to memorize. If only he had Pearl's memory.

Third period. Dutch was in math? No, science.

Adam started toward the science room.

He dashed down the hallway and stopped in front of the science room. "Hi, Mrs. Turner," he said, grinning at the teacher. "Mr. Parmar needs to see Dutch in his office."

Once Dutch had joined Adam in the hallway, Adam handed him his phone.

"What's going on?"

"I need you to call Ms. Gingko and pretend you're a teacher . . . Mr. Franco, maybe? Say that you're sending a boy to come down to clean up Parmar's office as punishment."

"What?" Dutch asked. "What went wrong?"

"I'll explain in a minute. Just call. If we don't get the new video uploaded, then we can't get Hill."

Dutch took the phone and dialed the number that Adam recited. "What's Mrs. Gingko's name?"

"Her desk says *Deborah*, but I think she goes by *Debbie*."

Dutch paused then said, "Umm, hello, Debbie? This is Mark Franco. There's a boy coming to the office in a minute. As punishment for being late to my class *again*, I'm making him clean up Mr. Parmar's office for his new desk. I talked to Bob and he said that would be fine."

Adam heard a higher voice on the other end but couldn't make out what she said.

"Yes, I understand. Thank you. Meeting? Oh yes . . . yes, the meeting. Uh . . . got to go. Bye."

Dutch clicked the phone off. "How was that?"

"Did she fall for it?"

"Seemed to," he said, shrugging.

"That's all we can do." Adam dropped his phone in his pocket. "I'm going to hang around the office and make sure Perk doesn't get stuck in there."

"Good luck," Dutch said.

Adam dashed back down the hallway. "Thanks for the help," he called over his shoulder.

He hoped this worked.

CHAPTER 49
Perk

Adam had made it happen.

He didn't know how, but when Perk walked into the office, Mrs. Gingko, peeling apart an orange, told him to go right in. "And make sure you are respectful with his belongings. I'm warning you that he knows everything in his desk, so no funny business."

"Don't worry," Perk said, and walked in, closing the door behind him. No computer out in the open like he'd hoped. Perk rifled through everything, looking for a computer bag or a briefcase. His fingers itched to look through the files he saw stacked along the wall, but he resisted. Another time. Right now, there was only one thing he needed to find.

Bingo.

A black bag sat behind Parmar's chair and Perk pulled out the thin metallic laptop. He logged on, pulled the camera out of his pocket, and connected it to the computer. He uploaded the file, making sure to give it the same name as the real video. A box popped up. "Hill Application Video already exists. Replace existing file?" Perk clicked Yes.

"I'm back, Debbie."

Parmar's voice.

Perk froze.

What had Adam said to Mrs. Gingko?

"I thought you were going to start putting things away for me," Mr. Parmar said. "I don't want to waste my whole day arranging everything. Besides my car is due for a wash."

The doorknob turned as Perk started for the window. It was the only way out.

"What? What phone call?" The shadow of Parmar's feet underneath the door retreated as Mrs. Gingko said something else.

Perk lifted the window and started to climb out. He stopped. Adam had somehow gotten him in, so he needed to be there. Right? He turned from the window just as Parmar pushed open his office door and said, "Who's the kid?"

"Uh, hi, Mr. Parmar."

"Oh, it's you. You're Percy, Perry, Pritens?"

"Perkins, Mr. Parmar. I was . . . " What had Adam told Mrs. Gingko? "Sent down here."

The principal looked around the room. "Well, it doesn't look like you've done anything. Franco's an idiot. Get back to class."

"Oh . . . okay. Thanks." Not wasting any time, Perk rushed out of the office. Mrs. Gingko was on the phone and glanced up at him. He started down the hallway.

"Hey!"

Mrs. Gingko. He pretended he didn't hear her.

"Hey, you!"

His heart skipped. He stopped then turned. "Yeah?"

She held out a citrus-dotted hall pass to him. "You'll need this to get back into Mr. Franco's class."

Perk sighed. "Oh, yeah. Um . . . thanks. I forgot."

She turned on her heel, and Perk ducked down the next hallway. Adam was leaning against the wall by the water fountain, waiting. He stood up when he saw Perk.

"Were you able to do it?" he whispered.

Perk nodded. "Yep. It's uploaded and ready to go."

They high-fived each other.

"Do you think he'll look at it before he sends it?"

Perk crossed his fingers. "Let's hope not. Now we just wait."

CHAPTER 50
Adam

Adam met Perk at his locker after school. "Did you hear about the recital tonight?"

Perk pulled an apple from his backpack before zipping it shut and slinging it over his shoulder. "No. Is Pearl in it?"

"Yeah. I didn't know, either, but I overheard someone mention it last period. We should go."

"Definitely. And maybe we can test out the codes for the doors. I don't have them yet, but I'll look them up when I get home." They started down the hall and pushed through the front doors.

"Good thinking. I'll call everyone and let them know."

"Yeah, okay." Perk bit his apple.

"You should bring Tommy," Adam said.

Perk shrugged. "Maybe. He hasn't been feeling well."

"Bummer. Did he go to school today?"

"No, you know how it is when he's sick."

Adam started off down the opposite sidewalk. "Well, hopefully he'll be able to make it."

"Sure. I'll see you later on tonight. What time does it start?"

"Seven."

"See you then."

When he got home, Adam grabbed himself a leftover donut and some milk. He took them to his room and then dialed Dutch's number.

"Hello, Walker residence," an old, wrinkled voice said.

"Hi. I was wondering if I could talk to Dutch? This is Adam, his friend from school. You took me home one time."

"Oh, I did, did I? Well, I wish I could say that Dutch was here, but he isn't. He walked down to the store for some soup. I can have him call you back?"

"He can call back if he wants to. But could you just tell him that we're going to the school tonight at seven for Pearl's concert?"

"Concert? Oh that's wonderful. Maybe I'll tag along."

"Great. Thanks, Mr. Walker."

"You bet. Seven at the school."

"Yep. Bye."

"Bye now."

He'd already talked to Perk and no need to call Pearl. He dialed Ray's number.

"Hello?" The voice on the other end was low and gruff, a lot like Ray's but older sounding.

"Hi. Can I speak with Ray, please?"

"Who's this?"

"Uh . . . Adam. I'm a friend of Ray's."

The voice laughed. "Friend? Really?"

For a moment Adam didn't really know what to say. "Yeah. Can I . . . can I talk to him?"

"Sure, Ray's friend." There was a pause and then a few expletives followed by "RAY! Get out here. You've got a friend on the phone. But don't be on long, okay?"

Adam listened as there seemed to be some sort of

struggle, an "OUCH!" and then a breathless voice answered, "Hello?"

What was going on? "Hey, Ray," Adam said. "This is Adam."

"Oh hey." The words came out fast and choppy like they were afraid to be held down.

"Who was that? Your dad?"

"No, brother. What's up?"

"Um." Why was he calling again? "Oh yeah. Pearl has a concert tonight at seven and I thought we should probably go. Maybe we can measure the roof or something while we're there?"

"Uh, yeah . . . about the car."

Pause.

"What about it?"

Yelling started from somewhere in the background.

"Never mind, I can tell you tonight."

"Tell me what?"

"I'll just see you there."

"Cool. So, I guess just dress up a little. Perk will have the—"

"Sorry, Adam." The yelling was louder, closer. "I gotta go."

The phone clicked off.

What was that about?

He swiveled around in his desk chair and stood up, trying to ignore the feeling inside his stomach. Ray was all right. He was sure of that. Right?

And the prank with the car was a go. Ray probably just had a question about something.

Right?

CHAPTER 51
Perk

Perk clicked off the phone and then turned on his computer. He jumped from one file to the next on Mr. Parmar's home screen, searching for the school codes.

"Do you want to play a game of Monopoly, Perk?" Tommy asked. He held out the half-torn game box. "Please, please, please." Tommy had stayed home sick that day with a cold and a cough. He stood there, his nose running and his lips chapped to a deep red.

"Maybe later, Tommy," he said, turning back to the computer. "I have to go to Pearl's recital in a little bit; we don't have time to start a game." Where were they?

"Can I go to the recital? I've never been to one before. I feel good. Watch."

Perk didn't turn around but clicked on another file. It had to be here somewhere. He remembered seeing it. "What?"

"I'm fine. I wanna go, too."

"Just a second." He was close; he felt it. Perk clicked on one document after another in the School Documents folder.

Tommy tapped him on his shoulder, but Perk held up his hand for him to wait. He grinned at the codes that popped up. "Bingo."

"Perk!"

There was a sudden crash behind him and Perk spun around in his chair. "Tommy! What are you doing?"

The Monopoly game—all the paper money, the pieces, the cards for Community Chest and Chance, and all the little houses and hotels were scattered across the floor.

"What did you do that for?"

Tommy wiped at his runny nose. "You weren't listening to me!" he cried.

Perk bent down and started picking up the pieces. "I was doing something. You have to be patient."

"You're always doing something! And I want to go to Pearl's recital! I'm going!" He crossed his arms across his chest.

Perk looked up at his brother, exasperated. "Well, you can't, Tommy. You're sick and you need to stay home and rest. Mom and Dad will be home soon; maybe they'll play with you?"

"No, I want you to play with me. You need to stay home."

"I can't. I have to go. It's really important."

"You're mean!" Tommy kicked the board and then tromped back to his room, slamming the door behind him. Perk could hear him start to cry.

Perk cleaned up the game, stuffing everything unceremoniously into the box. He glanced down at his watch, then back toward Tommy's room where he was crying harder.

The front door opened. "Perk? Tommy? I'm home!" His mom. Perk got up and grabbed his coat.

"You leaving to meet your friends?" she asked, setting down her briefcase.

"Yeah. I won't be long. Tommy's pretty mad that he can't come."

His mom patted him on the back. "Don't worry. Dad and I will bring him around."

"You could make him chocolate milk?" Perk suggested. "He'd love that."

"That's a good idea. Now you go and have fun. I'm glad that you're getting out with your friends a little more."

"Uh, yeah. Thanks." He wanted to say that Tommy was his friend, too—his best friend—it was just because Tommy really wasn't feeling well.

But instead he grabbed his jacket and jogged toward the school.

He'd be back before Tommy was even asleep.

CHAPTER 52
Ray

It was intermission and Ray was standing on the school roof.

Adam stood below him, his shadow long in the parking lot lights. Dutch hadn't shown up, so Perk was the lookout by the maintenance room in case someone wondered why the door to the roof was open.

Ray stretched the tape measure down the outside wall of the school to Adam, but he already knew the height. Fifteen feet.

"I can't reach it," Adam called up. "Lower it down farther."

Ray got on his knees, scuffing the black pants he'd worn. Great. "Do you have it?"

Adam pulled at the tape. "Got it."

"What is it?" Ray called down.

"A little over fifteen feet," Adam said. "I'll meet you inside."

Adam's end of the tape measure snaked up into the end Ray held, and Ray made his way back down the ladder and into the maintenance room where Perk waited.

"You done?" Perk asked. He walked out into the dark hallway and shut the door. They started back to the auditorium.

Ray shrugged. "Yeah, fifteen feet."

Adam pushed through the front doors of the school and walked toward them. "So what do you think?" Adam asked Ray. "That isn't too high, right?"

"It'll be close." Ray rubbed his arm and winced as he ran across the bruise his brother had given him. He might as well get it over with. "I just don't know if it's going to work."

Even in the dim light of the auditorium he could see Adam's face fall and Perk's eyebrows furrow. They had been counting on him to find a way. "What do you mean?"

He had to keep going whether he wanted to or not. "My dad has some jacks that might work on getting it up to the roof—maybe—since the car won't fit on just one. They're not wide enough for the entire car, so the front will have to go on one and the back will have to be supported by another. Even if we're able to maneuver both the jacks up at the same time, there's a huge chance that the car will fall or at the very least get scratched or dented."

Adam clapped him on the back. "But it can be done?"

Ray shrugged. "We'll have to test it."

"Yeah," Perk said. He ran his hands through his red hair. "I think testing it is a good idea. Then we can see if we're going to have to come up with something different."

"Something like marshmallows?" Adam shook his head. "It's the lamest idea out there. Nothing is as good as this. We'll have to try and make it work." He looked up as the lights to signal the end of intermission blinked. "It's about to start. We'll talk about this later."

Ray knew that Adam didn't mean for the words to

fall heavy, but they did. They felt like weights resting on his shoulder. Sure, there was still hope they could pull it off, but Adam had never worked one of the jacks; he didn't see the way they jerked up and shimmied, not to mention the noise they made.

They found their seats. Ray's stomach constricted.

If it didn't work, he'd disappoint his friends. No one had ever believed in him like Adam, Perk, Pearl, and Dutch. He didn't want to be a disappointment.

But he would be.

And really, he was disappointing himself.

Only when Pearl began to play did he forget about it for a moment or two. She was good. Or at least she sounded really good. The notes her bow played across the strings filled the auditorium and reached out to him.

Music had always been his least favorite class in school and it was just background noise at his house or the shop. Nothing more. It wasn't that he didn't like it; he really hadn't thought about it before.

But what Pearl played and how she played made him think about it.

Like she was singing through all those strings and

telling everyone something, sharing a secret, giving them something.

She did not disappoint.

Would he ever know what that was like?

CHAPTER 53
Pearl

The ground had dropped away from underneath Pearl's feet. And even as she lay in bed, she still felt like she was falling.

She rolled over. She didn't want to look at the flowers the boys had given her at her recital. All the boys but Dutch, who hadn't come. But who cared about him or the flowers? She *had* cared; she'd thought it was sweet and nice. But that was before. After, her parents fought and took her to dinner and told her they were getting a divorce.

A divorce dinner.

A dinner with a divorce at the end of it. On the night of her recital.

Everything was different.

She was different.

There were two Pearls now.

Before-the-divorce-Pearl and After-the-divorce-Pearl.

Before-the-divorce-Pearl had played her violin pieces perfectly and Before-the-divorce-Pearl had been so excited when she found out that Adam, Perk, and Ray had come and Before-the-divorce-Pearl didn't even mind that Dutch hadn't made it or that they were also there to measure the school roof. Before-the-divorce-Pearl had loved bowing in front of the clapping crowd and seeing her parents sitting next to each other. Before-the-divorce-Pearl was excited to go out to dinner with her parents.

Then the divorce dinner happened.

And then After-the-divorce-Pearl was born and she didn't care anymore.

After-the-divorce-Pearl didn't care about the flowers that the boys had given her or about the plan to go to Ray's dad's garage or about Parmar or Hill.

After-the-divorce-Pearl hardly cared about anything at all.

And curling up in a ball on her bed in the dark was the only thing that she knew she could do.

CHAPTER 54

Dutch

1. Gramps had forgotten to give him the message until it was too late

2. It was too late to go to Pearl's recital

3. He missed the recital

"I'm sorry that I forgot, Dutch," Gramps said. "I didn't have a piece of paper to write it down on and then—" He stopped and coughed into his handkerchief. The handkerchief he never left home without. He never forgot that.

"It's fine," he said. Dutch turned away, sat down at the computer, and turned it on. It wasn't fine, but how could he tell him that?

But being mad or upset at Gramps was something

he had only felt a few times in his life—like the time he forgot to sign a permission slip for Dutch to go to the art museum with his fifth-grade class. Everyone went but him; he had to stay behind and shelve books in the leveled book room.

And he hated being mad at Gramps. He knew his grandpa wasn't feeling well and that he forgot things and that he really did love Dutch.

But he'd missed Pearl's violin recital. He didn't get to sit by his friends or hear Pearl play or stand up and clap for her or hand her flowers afterward. Real flowers, not paper flowers. The anger soured in his mouth.

Dutch went to the chat forum for relatives of dementia. He visited the site almost every single day now, even though he still had never posted anything. He liked looking at the different ideas people had on how to help their "loved one." That's always how they addressed them: "their loved one" or "my loved one."

But right now Dutch didn't care about routines, puzzles, games, exercise, and diet.

He clicked off the site.

"I'm sorry, Dutch," Gramps said again. He rubbed his wrinkled hands through his white hair.

Dutch stood up. He didn't want to hear an apology. Saying sorry didn't bring back the evening.

He walked into the tiny kitchen, took a pair of scissors and a stack of paper and cut what seemed like a thousand pieces of paper into squares. Now his grandpa would have something to write on when someone called, now Dutch would get a message from his friends. When he was done, he took the stack and set them by the phone. Then he took the top piece of paper, taped it to the phone and wrote in all capitals: REMEMBER TO GIVE DUTCH MESSAGES FROM HIS FRIENDS!!!!!!

He walked back into his room and turned off his light and lay staring up at the blackness.

He felt like blackness right then.

CHAPTER 55

Perk

Was he missing something? It was after school, and Perk surveyed his stuff again where he sat in the school library. Computer, power cord, backpack, homework, snack. His phone was beside him. Nope, he had everything. It was Monday and Tommy was at his school for his art class. Perk didn't have much time before he had to leave, but he'd make it if he ran. Meeting everyone at Ray's shop wasn't until later that night.

The thought scratched him like an annoying tag on one of his shirts.

He looked back down at his computer and reread the e-mail that Parmar had sent Mr. Charles W.

Braynard, Director of Admissions, Beaumont Camp for Boys that afternoon.

From: Bill Parmar
To: Charles W. Braynard,
Subject: Beaumont Camp for Boys

Dear Mr. Braynard,

I am following up on Hill Robert Parmar's application for Beaumont Camp for Boys for this upcoming summer.

My son, with his high academic achievements; his volunteer work at the special needs building, animal shelter, and nursing home; and his participation in extracurricular activities sets him above the other applicants, I'm sure.

I am also sure that his video interview further enlightened you about his impeccable upbringing and demeanor.

If you have any questions that I can answer, do not hesitate to e-mail me at the above address. Once approved, we will pay promptly.

Sincerely,
Bill Parmar
Principal, Anderson Middle School

Perk smiled at the letter. Mr. Braynard would definitely be enlightened.

But—ugh. The feeling that he was missing something still nagged at him. What was—

His phone pinged and a text message lit up the screen.

Where are you? School called to ask if someone meeting Tommy at home. He's upset. Hurry. Can't be home for another hr.

His heart hit the bottom of his stomach like his mom's homemade pizza—and his mom was horrible at any sort of cooking, most of all, pizza.

It was Tuesday, not Monday. Tommy didn't have art class after school.

Perk glanced down at the clock on his computer to double check, then started shoving things into his backpack. He was awful, horrible, terrible.

He should've been home to meet Tommy's bus a half hour ago.

One long half hour ago.

It might as well have been forever ago.

Brothers didn't forget brothers.

But Perk was the exception.

CHAPTER 56
Adam

Adam rode his bike back toward the restaurant, the bag of groceries for his mom hanging off the handlebars.

He smiled into the warm air. In just a few hours they were going to Ray's dad's garage to test the idea for the car with the pump jacks. It would work. They'd just have to be careful, that was all.

Then by next week—the day of the spring dance— they would have gotten Hill and Parmar back for what they did to Tommy and to Dutch and to all the other kids.

Adam stopped at the stop sign and looked down either side of the street, his gaze catching on the high school, where three people stood beside the yellow school bus.

He squinted to see farther.

Tommy?

It couldn't be.

And who was that with him?

Adam turned his bike and rode down the sidewalk, recognizing Tommy's bus driver and Mrs. Pell.

What was this about?

"Hey, Tommy," Adam said, hopping off his bike and letting it clang to the cement.

Tommy turned to him, his nose red and crusted with green mucus, his shirt chewed and wet around his neck. "Adam!" he cried, and hugged him.

"What's wrong, Tommy? Where's Perk?"

"I waited for a while at the stop," the bus driver said. "But then I called the school, finished the route, and brought him back here."

Mrs. Pell rubbed Tommy's back. "We just heard from Tommy's parents that Perk should be coming any minute, so we're just waiting here together, aren't we, Tommy?" She said more quietly, "He's been pretty upset."

Tommy shook his head. "That was my stop. My bus stop. It's where I'm supposed to wait for Perk. He told me to never leave until he comes. But he didn't come and now he won't know that I'm here. And I'm cold and I want a red gummy bear and I want to go home."

Perk didn't forget him. It couldn't happen. He said the Internet at his house was down until tomorrow morning when they were going to upgrade it. "I'm gonna check Parmar's e-mail in the library," he'd told Adam. "I'll be at Ray's later on."

Adam pulled out his phone. It was almost dead, but alive enough to text him.

Tommy's waiting at school. He's upset.

U coming?

He hit Send.

Tommy smeared his hand over his eyes and nose at the same time then nodded. "I want to go home now. Adam, can you take me home? You can take me home and Perk will be there."

"We have to wait for Perk to come here, Tommy, remember?" Mrs. Pell said.

"Yeah, Tommy," Adam said. "But maybe I can wait

here with you until he gets here?" He looked over at Mrs. Pell, who smiled and nodded.

Adam glanced down the street. His stomach twisted and tangled and tightened up. What if Perk had forgotten Tommy? Tommy let out another sob and leaned onto Adam's shoulder. "Come on, Perk," he said. "Hurry up."

CHAPTER 57

Ray

Sneaking out was easy. His dad and brother didn't care where he was or where he went as long as he was out of the way.

Walking to his dad's shop in the dark was fairly easy. He kept his head down and quickened his pace every time a car drove past.

Opening up the shop was easy. He had the alarm code and the keys and only turned on a few lights in the back when he arrived.

And even pulling out the lifts and the two old metal bumpers that he thought they could use to test their plan was fairly easy. It was just a bumper, but they could at least get the idea and see what they were working with.

And then checking the Internet at the shop when no one was there was easy. He was curious about the school roof. He hadn't thought about whether it could hold the car until he walked past the hardware store beside the shop. A couple months ago a late winter snow had caved in through part of the roof. They were still fixing it. Ray typed in "how much can a flat roof hold" into the search bar. Twenty-five to thirty pounds per square foot. He typed in "weight of Shelby Cobra." Enter.

Two thousand, five hundred fifty pounds.

His heart plummeted.

The car would fall right through. Maybe not right away, but definitely by the time they figured out a way to get it down.

Nothing else about tonight was going to be easy.

Stupid. Why hadn't he thought of that before? Engineers thought about those sorts of things. He clicked off, stood up, and shoved back the chair. It banged into the filing cabinet behind him. Everyone would be here within a few minutes.

He wheeled the lifts into the open space and dragged the bumper over.

Even if it was easy to lift the bumper up with the levers, they were talking about a car that weighed two thousand, five hundred fifty pounds, a car that was worth almost six hundred thousand dollars, and a school roof that would be as flimsy as a piece of thin ice.

He wanted the plan to work; he wanted it to be easy. He really, really, really did.

He had friends now.

Friends who believed in him.

He had backup.

He was somebody else's backup.

But the plan *wouldn't* work.

And it wasn't going to be easy for everyone to find that out.

CHAPTER 58

Pearl

DA-na, DA-na, DA-na-da-na-da-na-da-na-da-na . . .

The theme music from *Jaws* played louder and faster inside Pearl's head and her fingers flicked faster and faster across the imaginary E and F strings as she walked around Ray's dad's shop. It felt like any moment, something was going to reach out and grab her.

She almost hadn't come tonight. She really didn't *want* to come tonight.

Her house was dark and quiet, so sneaking out wasn't a problem, but After-the-divorce-Pearl didn't care. Her parents were sleeping in separate beds in separate rooms and soon separate houses and she was supposed to be excited about getting a car on a roof?

Adam walked in, whispered something to Perk, then said, "Hey, Ray." She watched Perk shake his head and clenched his jaw.

"Hey."

And where was Dutch? Did he quit everything all together?

Just then he pushed through the front door. "Hey, guys."

"Hey," Ray said. He looked around. She could tell he didn't like even the smallest spotlight. "This is my dad's shop."

Adam nodded. "Cool. So, where are the lifts?"

"Uh, over here." Ray walked across the shop and Pearl followed along with everyone.

"You okay?"

Pearl glanced over at Dutch. She pasted a smile on her face—the one she used when she didn't want to talk to anybody. "Yeah, fine."

It should've made her feel better—that's what he was trying to do—but instead it just annoyed her. How much could he really care? He hadn't even bothered to come to her recital.

"I'm sorry I missed your recital the other night," he said, almost reading her mind. "My grandpa forgot to give me the message."

"It's fine. I don't care." She didn't. Really.

"But I really wish I could've heard you play." She didn't answer and he continued. "My grandpa's been forgetting a lot of things lately."

"Really?" She was paying attention and not. She cared. She didn't care.

"Yeah. I guess early signs of dementia, maybe. I don't know."

She turned and looked at him. "Wow. That's hard."

He shrugged. "Yeah." He squinted. "You don't seem fine, either. It's okay to not be fine."

He might've wanted to spill his guts, but not her. She brushed past him, nearly tripping over a long cord that ran the length of the dark shop. "But I *am* fine. Really."

"Be careful," Ray said, turning around. "There's a lot of stuff in here."

"I'm fine," she said again. How many times did she have to say it?

"Here's the jacks."

Pearl had seen things like this before on the side of the highway, men in hard, orange hats thirty feet in the air changing the picture on a billboard, or maybe she'd seen someone cleaning a window on one of them.

How in the world was it going to do what they needed it to do? What were they even doing? She heaved a sigh.

Dutch kept glancing over at her.

"What?" It came out meaner than she meant it to, but whatever. Maybe it would give her some space. Adam, Perk, and Ray were already starting to argue.

Dutch shrugged and looked away from Pearl. "It just seems like there's something wrong. And I . . . I don't know. I want to make you smile."

Pearl forced another grin. "Okay, I'm smiling, see. Besides, you don't seem 'fine,' either."

Dutch shrugged and directed his gaze back to the others.

"So this is it?" Adam asked.

Ray nodded and ran his hands along the top of the contraption. "We'll have to use two. One at the front end and the other at the back. One of us can work the one and someone else the other, then we'll need two people on flashlights and someone in the middle to make sure they're going up at the same time. The key will be in getting the car on both lifts using a jack and then working them so they go up at the same time. But—"

Ray was about to continue when Perk, who was walking around the two lifts, interrupted. "And the car will fit?"

"It'll fit, but barely. We'll have to be really careful. We don't want to scratch the paint or dent anything. But the thing is—"

"We'll be careful."

Ray sighed.

"Hey guys," Pearl said, "listen to Ray; he's trying to say something."

"What is it?" Adam had one of the remotes in his hands, and Pearl could tell he was anxious to try it out.

Ray coughed into his hand. "Well, the thing is, I'm not sure if the prank is gonna work."

"We'll go slow when we're using the lift," Adam said. "And we can practice. Don't worry about it. Now Perk, get on the other side of the lift."

Ray stopped Perk. "No, it's not the lift. It's the roof. The school roof."

"The roof?" Perk said. "You guys measured it. Did you get it wrong?"

Adam bristled. "I didn't get it wrong. Fifteen feet. I can read."

"I never said you couldn't—"

This time Ray interrupted. "I don't think the school roof can hold the weight of the car."

Silence echoed through the shop.

Pearl and Dutch looked at each other. Was he serious?

"It's a roof," Adam said. "It should hold a ton of weight."

"No, it doesn't. Spread out over the whole roof, yes, but all in one area like the car?" Ray shrugged. "I think it would fall right through. I just looked it up tonight."

"We put it on another roof then? Parmar's roof? The high school roof, above the room Tommy's program uses?"

Perk laughed. "Yeah, right. I doubt it's any stronger than the middle school roof. It'll fall through like cardboard."

"Well, this is great to find out now," Adam said.

He shoved the remote at Ray. "When were you going to tell us about this, Ray? Break the news next week when the car was on the jacks?"

Ray shrugged. "No. And I told you, didn't I?"

"Yeah, but you were about to let us start practicing with the lifts, and . . . and we're a week away from doing the prank."

"I don't know; I didn't want to ruin it for everyone. You guys were counting on me."

"Yeah, we were," Adam snapped.

"Leave him alone," Dutch said. Pearl pointed her flashlight over at him. He squinted a few times in a row. "Let's just put the lifts back and get out of here. Ray, lock up like nothing happened. We'll figure something else out."

Adam kicked a screw lying on the ground. "Oh yeah? What do you know about it, Dutch? Nothing. So just shut up."

"Hey," Pearl said. "Stop it. He didn't do anything."

"I know. Ray should've found out at the beginning so we weren't a week out with nothing."

Perk sighed. "It's fine. Don't worry, Adam, we'll make something work."

"Yeah? Like what?" Adam said. "Stupid sticky notes on his car?"

"Maybe. What's your obsession with putting it on the roof?" Perk said. "You're forgetting that this is about Tommy and getting back at the Parmars, not how cool the prank can be."

"Forgetting? I don't think you can talk, Perk. I'm not the one who left my brother on the side of the road."

"It was an accident—"

"Hey, cut it out, guys," Pearl said. "You know what, just forget it."

"I'm sorry," Ray said.

Pearl tossed her flashlight at Adam, who barely caught it. "I'm leaving. This is stupid. We're all going to get caught and the whole thing is over." She didn't turn around to hear any replies or see if anyone was following her.

They were all stupid boys.

And this was a stupid idea.

CHAPTER 59
Dutch

Why did he even agree to this?

Why did he let himself like Pearl?

Why did he let himself think that maybe she blushed because of him?

Why did he let himself like any of them?

Having his head dunked in the toilet was much easier. . . or at least less painful.

CHAPTER 60
Adam

He let the door slam behind him and started down the sidewalk. Pearl was already a block away.

This was what he got for asking everyone to join in on something that he and Perk could've done on their own.

But they couldn't have done it on their own.

He knew that, and that's why it was all so stupid.

And he hadn't forgotten what this was all about. He just wanted this to be the best—the coolest—prank they'd ever done.

For Tommy, of course. It was for Tommy and the others.

Adam rubbed his temples, his head aching.

CHAPTER 61
Perk

He hadn't meant to leave Tommy.

He hadn't meant to forget.

Adam was the last person that he wanted to find Tommy standing on the sidewalk, but then again, he was the only person he'd want to find Tommy.

And now everyone else knew.

His stomach turned.

If it had just been he and Adam, none of this would've happened, but then again, he wouldn't have three more friends.

He rubbed his eyes. Everything was blurry, jumbled up, and out of focus.

And he wasn't sure if he could find the answer—or if he even wanted to.

CHAPTER 62
Ray

The front door to his house was locked. The key under the mat was gone.

He walked to the side of his house and opened the window, hefting himself up and through and landing with a hard thump on his shoulder. He pushed himself up and leaned against the wall.

Wow. That couldn't have gone any worse.

But what did he expect?

Adam and Perk had asked him to join because they suspected that he was smart.

But he wasn't smart enough.

Some things never change.

CHAPTER 63
Pearl

She was lucky that her dad slept so deep. The back door barely whined when she opened it, padded through the kitchen, and saw him sleeping on the couch, a blanket pulled over him.

It was real.

He was really leaving, and everything that night had really happened, and the people who she thought were friends were the same as everyone else—no one listening, everyone just thinking about what they wanted and what they thought.

Pearl walked to her room, closed the door, and then fell on her bed without changing out of her clothes.

What did it matter?

CHAPTER 64
Adam

He felt like an idiot.

Not an every-day-regular sort of idiot, but a special-one-of-a-kind-egotistical idiot.

A Hill Parmar sort of idiot.

But at least he hadn't posted a picture of himself as his home screen. That was something, right?

But maybe that was the next step into becoming a special-one-of-a-kind-egotistical idiot.

It was an hour after he'd walked home and he hadn't slept. The clock on his phone moved from one number to the next, but he couldn't settle his mind enough to sleep. The scene replayed in his head.

The hero in stories always has this sort of choice—to

become what he's hated and fought against the whole time, or recognize that he's made a huge, humongous, enormous, egotistical-jerk-sort-of-mistake and he needs to make it right.

So, Adam had to choose either the egotistical-idiot route, or sorry-I've-been-an-idiot route.

He picked up the phone and dialed Perk's number.

CHAPTER 65
Perk

It was like a thick book had landed on his head and woken him up, and all in all he was glad for it. Not for the fighting with Adam or any of the others, or the fact that everything might be a wash now, but because he'd at least woken up.

Perk opened Tommy's door and glanced at him sleeping, the rising and falling of the comforter. He was snoring—Tommy was a terrible snorer.

He closed it again and almost wished it was morning. That he could wake up Tommy and they could watch some morning cartoons together and eat their cereal on the coffee table and then he could take Tommy out for dessert at Bakers' Place and Tommy wouldn't remember that Perk didn't meet his bus today and Perk would forget, too.

Tommy's face, puffy from crying and his nose running, flashed in Perk's head again. And again.

Perk went to his room, shrugged out of his clothes, and stared up at the ceiling. He had to make it up to Tommy. His cell phone hummed from its place on his dresser.

"Hey."

"Hey, Adam."

"So," Adam said. "I was a pretty big idiot."

"Yeah. Me, too."

"You still think we can make this work?"

"I'm in. It'll have to be different, but yeah." Perk paused. "Do you think everyone else is in, too?"

"Maybe we should do it on our own?"

"I don't know. We should think about it."

"Cool. I'll see you at lunch tomorrow?"

"See you then."

The phone call ended and Perk plugged it into his charger.

Pearl had been distracted. The confidence Ray had started to have had disappeared. Dutch was quiet and sulky. Adam was . . . Adam.

Maybe they all had needed a little wake up.

CHAPTER 66
Adam

Going it alone—only he and Perk pulling off the prank—seemed like the best way to go.

No mess. No chance of getting caught.

It was better.

"We need them, Adam," Perk said at lunch. "Besides, they've helped with everything from the beginning. It'd be wrong to cut them out now."

Adam shrugged and stuffed his uneaten sandwich back in its Ziploc bag. He couldn't eat.

He knew he had to apologize to everyone—he couldn't stop thinking about it.

"So, are you going to talk to them?" Perk asked.

The bell rang and Adam grabbed his lunch bag,

thankful that he could get away with a short response. "We'll see."

Yet again, Mr. Franco, Adam's gym-teacher-turned-fairy-godfather, was the one who swayed him one way.

It wasn't his quote, "A clear conscience is a sure sign of a bad memory," which he had spouted while they were practicing basketball passes and which had absolutely nothing to do with anything about passing or basketball or gym class or motivation. And it wasn't his "if you hit the target every time, it's either too near or too big," which didn't make a whole lot of sense either except if he thought about the target being the basketball hoop . . . though that still didn't make sense. It was his "no team works without teamwork" and "leave no man behind" that made the difference.

Perk was right; they needed everyone.

Even though it wasn't going to work out like Adam wanted, Ray had thought about how to do the car on the roof from beginning to end. What if he hadn't found out about the weight and they put the car up there and it plunged through the school? Pearl had become a spy at her own lunch table to help find out information, and even if it meant being humiliated by Hill on purpose, Dutch had always been willing to do whatever they needed. In fact, Adam and Perk had the least risk in all of this.

Yes, they needed everyone else, but not because they needed help. Because they were in it together.

CHAPTER 67
Perk

"Is it almost time to go, Perk?" Tommy asked.

"Almost, Tommy," he said. He rifled through his drawer, searching for something that was clean. "Are you dressed yet?"

Tommy tapped him on the shoulder, and Perk turned around. His brother was dressed in his suit and bow tie, the blazer pulling around his belly just a bit and the pants a little on the short side. He smiled wide and held out his arms. "How do I look?"

Perk grinned and high-fived Tommy. "You look awesome."

Tommy lifted up his chin a little. "Do you think Nish and Mrs. Pell will like it?"

"Of course." He glanced down at his watch and then at the flyer for the Special Education Art Show. "Now, what should I wear, Tommy? A plaid shirt and jeans?"

Tommy smiled. "No. You should wear your suit and bow tie, too. Then we'll be like brothers even though we're brothers already."

Perk hated getting dressed up and he especially hated the choking bow tie and the too-tight pants that his parents made him wear to synagogue. And not to mention the fact that he and Tommy would be the most overdressed kids at the art show. Hands down.

Still.

"Where's Mom and Dad?"

Perk put his hand on his neck, already feeling the tie choking him. "They're going to meet us there, remember? They wanted to have a car at your school so we could get ice cream afterward."

"Oh yeah! I love ice cream."

"I don't have to wear the bowtie, do I?" Perk asked, holding it up.

Tommy dragged him down the hall. "Come on. We don't want to be late. Get dressed."

And fifteen minutes later, Perk and Tommy were walking down the sidewalk to the high school, all dressed up in their suits and bow ties.

And even though the bow tie *was* choking his neck and the pants still felt too tight, Perk didn't mind.

"Pearl and Ray and Dutch and Adam are going to come, too," Tommy said, jumping over a crack in the sidewalk.

He should've warned Tommy earlier. "Adam will definitely be there, but I don't know about the others. But don't worry, there'll be a lot of—"

"No," Tommy said. "They told me they were coming."

Perk sighed. "Yeah, but that was a while ago. They might not have remembered."

"I e-mailed Pearl because my throat was sticky when I tried to call. She e-mailed back and said she would come. And I called Ray and Dutch. Ray didn't pick up the first time and then he did. They were excited to come."

Perk laughed. "How did you get their e-mails and phone numbers?"

"I looked on your phone and your computer. You

think I don't watch sometimes, but I do."

Perk wrapped his arm around Tommy's thick shoulder and pulled him closer. "I'm impressed, Tommy. Seriously, you're a smart guy."

Tommy leaned his head on Perk's shoulder for a moment before pushing off and dodging another sidewalk crack. "I know, Perk."

The front of Tommy's classroom greeted them with a bright banner that said, "Art Show." The special ed program had held at least six other fund-raisers that year to raise money to help remodel the main classroom, and the art show was another attempt. From all the work that still needed to be done, it seemed like the fund-raisers must not bring in much. Maybe something was better than nothing?

"Look, Perk," Tommy said, pointing to the banner. It was dotted with handprints and students' names written in different colors. "There's my hand. It's one of the biggest ones. Do you see that? I'm one of the biggest."

"That is pretty cool," Perk said.

They stepped into the building and walked down the hallway to the art room. Mrs. Pell smiled as they walked up. "Are you ready, Tommy?"

"Yes," he said. He twisted his shirt around and around his finger.

"Well, go on in and show your brother your painting and then you can wait for the other art lovers to come."

"Thanks, Mrs. Pell," Perk said, walking in.

Tommy showed him his painting, and though Perk was a little biased, his brother's was definitely the best. The house he'd painted was bright and smiling and so were the sun and trees. "This is so amazing," Perk said. "I'm impressed."

Tommy grinned. "I tried really hard. I cried when I drew that part because I messed up a little bit." He pointed to one of the trees, which had a little bit of brown and purple smeared. "But then I covered it up."

"I think it's perfect."

Perk looked toward the door and crossed his fingers. He hoped they all came.

CHAPTER 68
Ray

The classroom was thick with people, music trilled static-y from an old stereo set up on a desk, and even with the fan blowing overhead and the windows opened, Ray was already starting to sweat.

Luckily he'd remembered deodorant.

He spotted Tommy right away, showing his painting to Pearl while Adam and Perk stood off to the side looking at another painting. Dutch was at the refreshment table pouring himself a glass of punch. Ray swallowed, his own throat going dry.

He walked around the room in the opposite direction. He'd see Tommy's painting last, and then he'd leave and get a drink at the water fountain since he forgot to bring money for food.

He started around the semicircle of art and smiled at the proud artists standing beside their work—some shy and smiling, others serious and proud, and some who hid behind their hands every time someone walked by.

In between the painting of a rainbow and a painting of a dog, Ray realized Hill was there. His insides constricted and twisted; his fist tightened, but he stood back a little, not wanting to draw attention to himself.

"This is good, Nish," Hill told the girl standing next to her painting.

Ray's eyebrows raised. Had Hill actually complimented someone? The girl smiled and covered her hands with her face.

And then Ray heard Hill make a quiet, barely-there bark and then a whine—it sounded just like a dog.

What was he doing?

He continued, getting a little louder, when the girl—Nish—burst into tears.

Hill smiled and then turned away just as the girl's parents walked over to her. Adam, Perk, Tommy, Dutch, and Pearl all looked over as well.

"What's wrong, sweetie?"

The girl wailed even louder. "Why did he die? I didn't want him to die. He was my best friend. But then my dog died and went to heaven."

This is what Tommy had told him about.

As if watching it all on the outside of his body, Ray saw himself grab Hill by the collar, fling him around until Hill's surprised face looked into his, and then his fist pulled back and released like a catapult.

There was a crack as his fist connected with Hill's nose.

And then Ray saw blood.

CHAPTER 69
Pearl

She had never seen someone punch someone else in real life—only in movies.

And though it happened mostly the same as what she'd seen on the big screen, there was more blood and this blood was real and the chaos around the blood was real.

But she didn't feel real. The scene didn't feel real.

"He punched me!" Hill cried.

Mr. Parmar, who was talking to Tommy's teacher, rushed over. "What's going on? Oh my gosh! Hill? What happened?"

Pearl looked at Ray. His shirt was wet around his armpits. His cheeks flushed a deep red and his eyes, though they were fiery and rimmed with his furrowed eyebrows, had filled with tears that leaked out onto his face.

She never would have expected that.

"He was making that girl cry," Ray said. His voice trembled a little bit and he looked at his fist, wiping the blood smeared across his knuckles onto his jeans. "He was making dog noises and then she started to cry. He's done it before."

"It was just a joke," Hill said. "Gosh!"

"It wasn't a joke to her," Dutch said. His voice shook, too, and in addition to him squinting, his neck and cheeks filled with red.

"We don't know all the facts except that Hill's nose is most likely broken." Mr. Parmar put his hand on Ray's shoulder. "You get out of here before I call the police. We don't tolerate this kind of behavior in any part of our school system." He led Ray out the door. "I'll see you in my office in the morning, is that understood?"

Pearl watched Ray swipe at his face and then jog out of the school.

Parmar held out a paper towel to Hill, who winced

when he put it on his nose.

Hill said under his breath, "This is such a freak show."

The blood in Pearl's veins rushed through her.

She walked closer to him. "You're such a jerk. You need to apologize to her for what you did."

"What are you talking about, Pearl?" Hill said. "Are you standing up for him? For these losers?" The blood on the paper towel was seeping through. He leaned closer and continued, quieter. "I didn't know zebras like you would be so sensitive about everything—is that your black side or your white side? Is that what made your parents get a divorce?"

Her breath caught in her throat. "What?"

"Everyone knows, Pearl. And now you're a freak lover, too."

And she wanted to punch him. She wanted to push him.

But Dutch beat her to it.

CHAPTER 70

It felt good.

Really good.

He could almost feel Mr. Parmar's hand still gripping his shoulder and pushing him outside the classroom.

But he saw Pearl's smile, and Tommy's wave, and the way that Perk and Adam looked at him like Gramps did when he said, "I'm proud of you, Dutch."

"Your grandfather will be hearing from me tonight," Mr. Parmar said, pointing his finger at him. "You can't act like a savage around my son."

What would his grandpa say?

He was pretty sure that Gramps would understand

once Dutch explained it to him. But really, even if he didn't, shoving Hill wasn't something he could've stopped himself from doing even if he had tried.

The feeling of pushing Hill down and standing over him actually made his stomach turn. But the look on the others' faces was something he would never forget.

He had done something about what was happening in front of him.

His heart drummed inside of his chest.

Maybe he could do something about the swirlies and the lockers and the posters, too.

CHAPTER 71

Adam

Adam paced his bedroom a few times, then sat down at his computer and turned it on.

He stood up, walked to the window, then walked back. Sat down.

It was time to be creative, careful, precise.

Right up his alley.

He clicked on a few files on Mr. Parmar's computer, read them, then did more pacing to the window and sitting down again. The adrenaline from the art show was still running through his veins and, from the looks of the files he was pulling up, it was going to stay there.

Adam looked over the school budget estimates,

the actual budget right then, the different funding for school programs, and some back-and-forth emails between Parmar and one of the school board members about funding.

Adam laughed to himself.

It didn't take a rocket scientist to know what was going on. Mr. Parmar and a guy named Mike who was on the school board were taking money from the budget for the special education program. New football jerseys, a new desk for his office—the list kept going.

Adam attached the files to an e-mail, sent it off to Perk, and then texted him: **Check e-mail.** Then he sat back and waited for the call.

Sometimes things just needed a little tweaking. A science class with Mr. Spierling rather than with Mr. Hornblath, thirteen absences changed to eight. Some sorts of tweaking made things worse, like the time his mom decided to go a little blonder with her hair and ended up looking like his Aunt Hildy, while others made something better, like adding chocolate chips to banana bread.

And this tweaking needed to be the crème de la crème, the pick of the litter, the best of the best, the perfect tweak to an almost perfect plan.

When Perk called him five minutes later, he was fuming.

Adam, calm, creative, and precise, interrupted Perk's rant. "Let's come up with something new."

CHAPTER 72

Perk

Perk looked at the copy of tomorrow's morning announcements on his computer.

"Just be careful that you don't change it so much that Hill realizes it," Adam had told him.

The changes he made weren't exactly subtle, but they didn't need subtle right now; Perk couldn't do subtle right now. They needed a plan and they needed three other specific people.

He read through the announcements one more time, then sent it off to Adam.

Adam texted while Perk brushed his teeth.

ADAM: you sure about this?

PERK: yep

He printed off the paper and set it on his backpack so he wouldn't forget in the morning. Then Perk climbed in bed. He still couldn't settle down.

Every part of him was twitchy—nervous, excited, angry. The covers were too hot on his body but his feet were too cold without them, so he lay with everything bunched up around his feet.

He stared up at the dark ceiling.

They only had a few days to pull it all together.

CHAPTER 73
Ray

He was forced to leave the school property after he punched Hill, and he was fine with that. Well, not totally fine, because he never did get to see Tommy's painting up close or congratulate him.

And he had scared himself.

It had happened so fast, his fist reacting before his mind had a chance to know what it was doing. He wasn't sorry about it, not when he thought of the girl crying or Hill chuckling to himself. But maybe he should be.

Without bothering to change his clothes, Ray fell onto his bed.

Would he hear from Adam or Perk?

The answer was immediate. It wasn't *if* he heard from Adam or Perk, it was a matter of *when*.

He'd just have to wait.

CHAPTER 74
Pearl

Pearl listened for the door to close below and when it did, the house echoed a bigger silence.

One that her dad didn't occupy anymore.

Her mom's voice carried from outside as she helped Pearl's dad load a few things into his car so that he could have some essentials in his apartment.

So that it could feel more like home?

But home was here. With her.

Silence. That was what played in her head right now for whatever this divorce thing meant. Her fingers didn't flicker across the imaginary strings and nothing played in her head. Her hands lay limp and lifeless.

Pearl turned her head toward the window when she

heard the trunk of her dad's car close. The headlights lit up her window from below as the car hummed to life.

Her parents hadn't fought once since they told her. Not once.

It was as if now that the decision was made, they were friends again.

The lights disappeared down the road, and she could picture him driving the five blocks straight, right on Hanford, first left into Riverside Apartments, Apartment 1C. Ten minutes away, if that. And there wasn't a river behind or beside or in front of the apartment building.

Pearl closed her eyes. Her mother's footsteps sounded down the hall and then her door opened.

"Pearl?"

She didn't answer. She didn't want to talk right now. There wasn't really anything to say anyway. She made her chest rise and fall rhythmically as if she were asleep. Thankful her mother couldn't see her eyes.

"I love you," her mother said.

The light from the hall disappeared and the door clicked shut. Pearl flipped onto her back and stared at the ceiling.

The night had been a long one. Weird and infuriating and good and awful.

Weird: going to Tommy's art show and seeing her friends there. And Dutch. But not talking to them.

Infuriating: Hill. In so many ways.

Good: Ray punching Hill and then Dutch pushing him.

Awful: A pizza dinner with her parents and then afterward her mom and dad packing up a few boxes.

Her dad closing the trunk and driving away.

CHAPTER 75

Dutch

1. Get up

2. Go to school

3. Hope that he and his friends—that was still how he thought of them—would make up

4. If they didn't, he would say something to them. He could do that now

"How did everything go with your friends last night?" Gramps asked at the kitchen table. He poured water into the jug of milk to make it last longer. "Did anyone come?"

Dutch tried to ignore the fact that his grandpa had asked him all of this in the car last night after the art show. "It went fine, I guess," Dutch repeated. "We actually didn't talk much, but it seems better."

He hoped so.

They hadn't really gotten the chance to talk at all. But some things, he was coming to think, didn't need to be said out loud.

Still, Dutch wasn't sure what to do next.

"Well, I wouldn't worry," Gramps said, interrupting his thoughts. "Good old-fashioned conflict is good for you. It'll make you all closer. Just give it time."

"Thanks, Gramps."

His grandpa sat down across from him at the table and sighed. "I already told you that, didn't I?"

Dutch nodded and smiled. "Yep, but that's all right. It's good to hear things more than once."

"And I already talked to you about fighting? About how I'm proud you stood up for someone but be smart about things like that?"

"Yeah."

Dutch shrugged into his coat and looked at the clock on the stove. He still had some time, but maybe he'd go to the bus stop a little early. He stood up. "There's nothing to be sorry about, Gramps. The doctor said there would be good days and bad, remember."

His grandpa gave him a smile. "Yeah, I remember that much." He stood up and wrapped Dutch in a hug. "Well, I'm proud of you, Dutch. And I love you. Remember that, okay?"

Dutch nodded. "I will. I love you, too."

And then he stepped outside and walked to the bus.

But things between he and his friends didn't seem better when he got to school. He didn't see Adam or Perk, but the others moved through the sea of kids opening and closing lockers like they had before. No one looked up at him. No one noticed. They all acted in an "I'm fine" sort of way.

In homeroom, he sat still, looking straight ahead.

But when the morning announcements crackled over the loudspeaker, things changed.

"Good morning, Anderson Middle School," Hill said too-loud over the loudspeaker.

Dutch wished that Jared was still in charge of morning announcements—everyone liked his corny jokes, music, and top ten lists every Friday. But when he had got too popular, Hill had taken over.

Hill blathered on and on, reading off the announcements of lost and found and after-school activities in his monotone, stilted sort of way.

"One last thing: to the students involved in the incident at the garage—and you know who you are."

What?

Dutch sat up, his heart racing. His face squinted up a few times in a row—he couldn't help it.

"Uh, to those students, we want to apologize for the incident and say that we hope you will all continue to be involved in the project. Friends stick together. And see, we can even make this egotistical Neanderthal say whatever we want. Hill eats poop for breakfast." There was a pause, then Hill continued, not realizing what he had just said. "Have a great day of learning."

The loudspeaker clicked off.

Everyone in Dutch's homeroom burst into laughter. His teacher called down to the office.

Dutch looked around and chuckled.

They were ready to go.

CHAPTER 76
Adam

Adam had never sat with Ray or Pearl or Dutch at lunch before.

Until today.

Dutch was the first to walk over and set down his tray. Then Pearl with her bag lunch and chocolate milk, and finally Ray stood by them, lunch tray in hand.

"Take a seat, Ray," Adam said.

Pearl stuck the straw in her milk container. "So what's the plan?"

Adam leaned forward, and wiped his palms on his jeans. He needed to say it. "Before we get into all that, I just want to say . . . I was a pretty big jerk the other night. I guess I just—" He shrugged. "I don't know, so yeah, sorry."

"It's all right," Pearl said. She smiled. "You *were* being a jerk, but I know I was out of it, too. I'm not sure if you heard Hill say something about my parents splitting up. Well, they did. My dad moved out. So, I guess you could say I wasn't really in the best mood." She let out a shaky breath, then took a long sip on her straw.

"Whoa, that's rough. I'm . . . really sorry."

"Yeah, sorry about that, Pearl."

"Hill's such a jerk."

She nodded. "Thanks, guys."

Dutch squinted. "Pearl's right. I was sort of out of it, too. I told Pearl, but you guys were busy with the lifts. My grandpa has the beginnings of dementia, so he's forgetting things a lot."

Adam remembered talking with Dutch's grandpa that night. He seemed perfectly normal. But obviously he wasn't. That was a scary thought.

"Well," Perk said. He smiled and gave a chuckle, but Adam watched as his face grew serious. "Since we're all baring our souls here, I forgot Tommy after school the other day. I hate that I did. I hate myself that I did."

"Perk, I'm sure he forgives you. It was a mistake," Pearl said.

He ate a salt and vinegar chip. "Yeah. Still."

"Ray," Adam said, saving Perk from the attention. "Do you want to bare your soul at all?"

"No, I'm good. I just want to figure out what to do to get the Parmars back."

Adam leaned forward and rubbed his hands together. "So you wouldn't believe what we found on Parmar's computer. It's bad. We need ideas and we need them fast."

CHAPTER 77
Perk

"What did you find out?" Ray asked.

Perk looked over at Adam. "Do you want to tell them?"

"After you." Adam gestured for him to go ahead.

He smiled and sighed, feeling as if he'd been holding his breath for too long. He was surrounded by his friends again. "Well, it turns out that Parmar and some other guy have been taking money out of the budget for the special ed program. A little here, a little there."

"What?" Pearl said. "You mean stealing money?"

Perk grimaced. "I think he'd probably call it 'moving things around.' But yes, stealing."

No one continued to eat and no one spoke.

That was the reaction he had hoped for—three other people, besides he and Adam, who were close to boiling over.

"Well, we need to tell someone," Dutch said.

Adam nodded. "We could. Or—"

Perk broke in. "We get creative and find a way to get the money back."

CHAPTER 78

Ray

Ray couldn't believe it.

Parmar was low, he'd known that for a while.

But this took *low* and gave it a new definition.

Still, besides telling someone about it, what were they going to do and how would that involve his car?

Ray took a bite of his sandwich. Parmar's car. His 1966 Shelby Cobra. Think. Think. Parmar's car.

And then he had it.

"We sell his car," Ray said.

Everyone turned to him.

"What do you mean?" Dutch asked. "Do you know what it's worth?"

Adam grinned. "I'm sure he does. Keep going, Ray."

Ray nodded. "We've seen his car a lot in the shop for waxing or other fix-ups. My dad was talking about it once. If I remember it right, it's worth about six hundred thousand dollars."

Perk dropped his fork. "What? Are you serious?"

"Six hundred thousand dollars?" Pearl echoed.

"Yeah. They're vintage cars and his is in really good condition." He stopped. "But how could we do it?"

"He could say it was a mistake and the whole thing will backfire."

"We could threaten him?" Dutch said. "Sort of like blackmail."

Adam shook his head. "That's good, but it leaves too much of a trail back to us." He tapped a carrot stick on the table. "Keep thinking, guys. This is good."

What would possibly make Parmar want to sell or give up his car? Nothing. He practically worshipped that car. "The main thing is that we're able to get the money to the special ed. program," Ray said aloud. "So Parmar needs to be involved for it to work."

CHAPTER 79
Pearl

"Wait," Pearl said. She smiled. Resting her mind on something other than her mom and dad, her two houses, two bedrooms, two lives, was a welcome relief. And the idea playing on repeat in her head just might work. "What if we—or Parmar—auction off his car?"

"How would that be different?" Dutch asked. "And why would Parmar auction off his own car?"

But Perk nodded. "Keep going."

"Well, Ray's right. The only way it's going to work is if he's in on it, but"—this was the part that she wanted to make sure she explained the right way—"he doesn't *know* that he's in on it until it happens."

"Huh?" This was from Ray.

"So you're saying—" Adam began.

Pearl cut him off. "If we auction off his car for charity—for Tommy's school—it would seem like his idea."

"But then he'd be the hero?" Dutch squinted. "We don't want that, right?"

"For a little while," Perk said, "but we could send the suspicious files and emails off to someone so it wouldn't stay secret for long."

"Yeah," Ray said. "We could tell the newspapers about it."

"I get it. So the special ed. program would have the money, and Parmar would be without his car. But he couldn't—or wouldn't—have the guts to take the money away from the special ed. program because everyone would think he was a horrible person." Dutch looked over at Pearl. "That's really good."

Pearl's heart did a staccato beat inside her chest. "Thanks."

CHAPTER 80
Dutch

The way Pearl smiled back at him flipped his stomach on end. There was no use in trying to keep his mouth and cheeks and eyes from squinting.

But he wasn't embarrassed and Pearl didn't seem to mind his tic.

But that was impossible, right?

So was standing up to Hill until a few days ago.

Ray opened his chocolate milk. "So who should call the newspapers? Wouldn't they be able to trace it to one of us or maybe treat it like a joke?"

Adam knocked him with his elbow. "Hey, Dutch. Can you do Hill's voice?"

Dutch swallowed a bite of his sandwich, closed his

eyes, and tried to hear Hill's voice in his head. "Hey Dork, what do you think you're doing with my homework in your backpack?" The words came out easy. He'd heard them enough. "How does that sound?"

Adam shook his head. "That was perfect. Pearl, do you think you could memorize some of the teacher's cell phone numbers?"

"Sure, why?"

"Just in case we need an out."

"All right."

Adam turned back to Dutch. "So what do you think of Hill calling the newspapers? You know, brag about his dad doing something really generous, blah, blah, blah."

"I'm in."

"That's good," Ray said. "He'll get in so much trouble with his dad. He probably won't even be allowed to go to that camp."

"True." Perk looked disappointed. "But maybe Parmar can put him in a different camp?"

"Remember Ray's idea about the military camp," Dutch said. This just kept getting better and better. "We could leave an application on his desk for him to find?"

"And Dutch could call and pretend to be Parmar," Adam suggested.

"He could," Perk said. "Though I don't think he'll have to."

"Why not?"

"Because," Dutch said, "once Parmar thinks that Hill told the media about his car, we could have an application to a Russian gulag and Parmar would gladly sign the papers."

CHAPTER 81
Adam

Adam glanced at his clock.

Two-thirty a.m., Friday morning.

It had been a busy few days, and he should've crashed into sleep, but all the what-ifs had made it impossible. He was still leaning against the headboard of his bed like he'd been doing since ten o'clock. Now it was time to get moving.

He sat up and grabbed his phone, then texted Perk and Pearl.

It's go time

He hit Send.

It was a chain reaction.

Perk was going to call Ray. One ring. And Pearl

was going to call Dutch. One ring.

He doubted any of them would forget, but they couldn't take chances.

Adam felt the zing of adrenaline through his veins. He stuffed his bed to look as if he was nestled under the covers, though he couldn't see either of his parents waking up—they slept like rocks. After dropping a flashlight, the walkie-talkies, plans, his cell phone, some candy, and a few other supplies into his backpack, Adam slipped his black hat on his head and lifted the window. He turned and took one last look to see if he had forgotten anything, then crawled out the window.

The sidewalks and streets were empty, illuminated by the circles of glowing light from the streetlamps.

His heart thudded inside his chest—a feeling which was relatively unfamiliar to him. He didn't get nervous about much, but it was different right now.

He was different right now.

He and Perk might have started this whole thing, but all five of them were going to finish it.

Picking up his pace, he started to jog.

CHAPTER 82
Perk

Tommy was asleep. His shoulders were rising and falling underneath his blankets, and his breathing was heavy. Perk's parents were upstairs on the second floor by the library. They wouldn't hear a thing.

Perk glanced down at his watch. He had fifteen minutes, plenty of time to get to Pearl's dad's apartment and meet up. He hoped the one ring was enough to wake Ray.

Perk had gotten everything ready before bed and had double-triple-quadruple-checked everything, so he slung his backpack over his shoulder and popped a piece of gum in his mouth—gum always kept him awake.

"We're going to make everything right," he whispered to Tommy's sleeping form. He thought of Nish and Dutch and William Bubert and Pearl and Ray, too.

This was their revenge.

Then he closed the door most of the way, just how Tommy liked it.

It was going to be awesome.

He wasn't worried at all.

Not really.

CHAPTER 83

Ray

The sky was a thick black when Ray opened his window and dropped to the ground. The TV was still blaring from the living room, but that's how his brother fell asleep most nights. Besides, he locked his bedroom door so no one could see that he was gone.

His heart was hammering and his mind and arms and legs were wired with energy. Everything had seemed so simple when they were planning it around the lunch table. Now, he was on his way to help break into Parmar's house and then the school.

They were crazy.

Ray stopped on the sidewalk and leaned his hands on his knees. He might throw up.

Breathe in. Breathe out.

They couldn't get caught.

He stood, took another breath in, and kept walking.

A month ago he wouldn't have cared. A month ago he didn't have friends and he was going to be a mechanic.

Now, who knew?

But the possibilities were exciting.

More than that, it excited him to know that there *were* possibilities.

CHAPTER 84

Pearl

It was weird to say good-bye to her mom at the door earlier that night.

That was probably the weirdest thing so far. Sort of like the violin piece that her teacher had her play called "Danse Macabre" by Camille Saint-Saëns.

It was creepy, and weird, and strangely beautiful, and completely confusing all at once.

That was definitely how she felt.

"I'll pick you up after school on Tuesday, okay?"

Pearl leaned into her mother's hug. "Okay."

Her dad's silhouette filled the doorway, blocking out some of the light that lit up the small, dark porch. "It was good to see you, Mary," he said.

She smiled and nodded. "You, too. And let me know if plans change, okay?"

Pearl let her dad answer.

"We will."

The door closed and Pearl turned around to go to her other home. She had two homes, now. Did anyone ever really get used to that?

Her room was small, but neat, with a window that faced the parking lot and a big tree right out front. She needed to bring some stuff over to make it feel more like her room, though. But what stuff?

How do you divide your room up between two homes? Clothes, pictures, memories?

Could memories be divided?

Or does one place become your real home and the other is a sort of vacation home?

Now, she shook her head and glanced out the window into the dark.

Two flashes.

"We should all meet at Pearl's house," Dutch had said yesterday.

"I'll be at my dad's apartment actually. I'm not that far. I can just meet you guys at the Parmars.'"

"No, we'll meet at the apartment," Adam said.

She'd never had any siblings, and now, she had four brothers who watched out for her.

She blushed and clicked her flashlight twice in reply.

It was a funny thing—how people she'd only known for a month could feel so close to her, and other people that she'd known since she was born could feel like she'd never known them at all.

Pearl grabbed her backpack and flicked off her closet light. Then she lifted the window and crawled out. Once she'd dropped the few feet to the ground, she ran to meet up with her friends waiting by the streetlamp.

CHAPTER 85
Dutch

He wiped his hands on his pants as Pearl ran up to where he and the others stood on the sidewalk.

Tonight was the night they were finally going to pull off the prank.

Dutch's heart pounded in his chest, much like how it did when Hill grabbed him from behind and hauled him into the bathroom or shoved him into a closet.

But there was no toilet bowl or closet rushing to meet him this time.

This was their night, his night.

They moved in the grass along the sidewalk, hoping to keep out of the light from the streetlamps.

"It's the third one on the left, right?" Ray whispered.

"Yeah, that one right there."

A fat tree stood in the yard, and the small porch light cast a shadow of the tree onto the road. "All right, guys," Adam said. "One more time."

He and Perk gave everyone the rundown of the night, even though they'd gone through it a zillion times already. They finished each other's sentences, just like they'd done that first day in detention.

Dutch grinned.

And as they stood in the dark, ready to go, Dutch's heart in his throat with excitement and nervousness and hoping that it would turn out right, he felt for Pearl's hand and held it.

He looked at her and squinted.

She squeezed his hand.

"All right. We're ready," Adam said. "Let's do this."

And when Pearl let go, Dutch knew that things had already turned out right.

CHAPTER 86
Adam

While Ray waited at the front of the house and Pearl and Dutch hid in the bushes in case something went wrong, Adam and Perk removed the spare key from underneath the mat on the back porch.

"You ready?" Adam asked. He slipped off his shoes and wiggled his toes. His fingers were shaking and even though he could feel a line of sweat trickle down his back, he shivered.

Perk nodded.

Summer was almost upon them, but the night air was still cool and Perk's breaths came out in small cloudy bursts in the darkness.

What were they doing? This was crazy.

"You okay?" Perk asked.

"Sure . . . yeah. It's bigger than anything we've ever done."

"I know." He took a deep breath in and Adam watched it puff out. "Are you ready?"

"Ready."

Adam gripped the key in his slippery fingers and slid it into the lock. He turned it slowly, easing the door open. His heart slammed against his chest and he motioned Perk inside.

"Pearl said the kitchen was on the right?" Perk whispered.

Adam pulled out a piece of notebook paper with a drawing on the front. Pearl was a violinist, definitely not an artist. "No, from her drawing, it should be on the left. I'll check by the front door and you check in the kitchen."

"Got it."

After clicking on his headlamp, Adam tiptoed across the kitchen in his bare feet to the small hallway by the front door. Coats hung right where Pearl had said they'd be, and there was the hook . . . with no car keys.

Adam sighed and searched each coat pocket for any sign of them.

Nothing. He had been afraid of this.

Adam met up with Perk at the back door. "Did you get them?" Perk asked.

"No," he whispered. He clicked off his headlamp. "They weren't there."

"Did you check the pockets in all the coats?"

Adam nodded. "Yeah, nothing in those, either." He paused, knowing what he had to do. "I'm going to have to go in his office."

"Really?"

"If they aren't here, then they must be there. Why don't you check in the coats again to make sure I didn't miss anything?"

"I'll search the office if you want?" Perk said. "Or I can go with you."

"No, I got it. But where did Pearl say it was?"

"She said it was down the hallway on the right."

"All right. Here goes nothing." He made his way through the hallway, found the first door on the right and pushed it open. He went to the desk and rifled through the drawers, finally finding a set of keys that were labeled "Spares." A keychain from Ray's father's shop hung off one key.

"Bingo," Adam said, and stuffed them into his pocket. Then he tiptoed out to meet Perk.

CHAPTER 87
Perk

Perk was hungry.

He usually was. But not necessarily in the middle of the night.

But now that he was up, walking around in the dark in Parmar's house, his stomach rumbled angrily.

Perk walked over to the refrigerator. A picture of a younger Hill and an old dog, gray around the muzzle—hung on the refrigerator. They had a dog?

He looked around. No food bowl or water dish.

The dog must've died. Why was Hill such a jerk about Nish's dog then?

Perk opened the refrigerator and squinted at the sudden burst of light.

Cheese. Leftovers. Milk. Eggs. A few apples rolled around, a container of yogurt, and a head of lettuce.

Perk smiled and grabbed an apple. "Don't mind if I do," he whispered.

"Perk," Adam whispered.

Perk closed the refrigerator door, looking down the hall, his eyes not quite adjusted to the darkness. "Adam?"

"Come on!" He stepped lightly along the floor until he reached the kitchen.

"Did you get them?"

Adam smiled and dangled the keys in front of him.

"Awesome." The first part of the plan was done.

Almost. They had the keys now, but they still needed to get the car out of the garage.

Perk followed Adam out of the house, careful to lock the door again behind him. Then they rounded the corner and met up with the rest of the crew, still melted in with the darkness.

"You got the car keys?" Ray asked.

"Yep. Now for the garage door."

"You're sure they won't wake up when it opens?" Pearl asked.

"No," Perk said. "Not entirely." There were no guarantees. He watched the windows, his heart speeding up as he waited for a light to flick on.

They had to hurry.

Ray piped in and held up Perk's iPhone, "I looked up their garage door, and it's a Whisper Genie Silent Max Two Thousand with a DC motor and a belt drive. It's pretty quiet. We'll have to do it manually."

"How?"

"We can get in by that door." He pointed to a door on the side of the garage. "Then there should be a red handle that hangs down from the top. You have to grab that and pull down. I can pull down while you guys lift the door from the outside."

Perk watched Ray disappear into the garage, the light of his headlamp bobbing through the little windows on the garage door. He bent down and gripped the garage door alongside Adam, Pearl, and Dutch.

Please don't be loud. Please don't be loud.

Ray's voice crackled over the walkie-talkie. "I've got the lever."

Perk lifted, feeling the door move up a little. "Here goes nothing."

CHAPTER 88

Ray

They stood silent for a few moments when the garage door was all the way open, staring into the windows of the house for any sign of lights being flipped on.

Nothing.

Ray let out his breath and caught the keys that Perk tossed to him.

"Ready?"

Ray grinned and inserted the key and unlocked the door.

It felt good to ease into the car, to shift the gear into neutral and steer it as everyone pushed it silently down the driveway away from the Parmars' two other cars and onto the street.

During the summers, when he spent most of his days doing whatever his dad asked him to do, Ray sat behind the wheel of the company truck grabbing lunch for everyone, picking up a part, dropping off a part, stuff like that. His dad made Ray promise that he'd go the speed limit and wouldn't bring any attention to himself. "And if you get caught," he'd say every time, "I'll pretend like I don't know anything about it. You hear me?"

He'd heard.

And now it was paying off. Maybe there was a reason for everything, or at least most things.

When they'd pushed the car down the road far enough, and the garage door was shut and still no lights came on in the house, Ray started the engine, feeling the rumble and roar underneath his feet.

They'd done it. Or at least part of it. Ray grinned. The car was one step closer to being auctioned off.

Pearl hopped into the front seat with Ray and shut the door while the others squeezed in the backseat.

"Are we ready?" Ray asked.

But he didn't need to hear their answer, even if he could've over the roar of the engine as he pressed the gas.

They were ready.

CHAPTER 89

Pearl

It was funny.

They'd been planning and talking about getting back at the Parmars for what seemed like forever. Now they were actually parked behind the school in front of the double gym doors and Perk was punching in the numbers to the alarm system and she and Dutch were holding them open and Ray was driving inside the school, and Pearl could hardly believe they were actually pulling it off.

Pearl grabbed a nearby rock and propped open one door and Dutch did the other, then Ray cut the engine of the Shelby Cobra and they all pushed it across the clean cafeteria floor, their sneakers squeaking.

She glanced at them and almost felt like crying.

But in a happy way. A "Hobo's Blues" sort of way.

A wow-we're-really-doing-this-and-thank-you-for-being-my-friends sort of way.

Dutch turned and squinted at her, maybe because of the headlamp light shining in his face, or maybe because of his tic.

Either way, it didn't matter.

CHAPTER 90
Dutch

1. Be quiet
2. Don't get caught

The school was quiet at night and Pearl was all smiles and excitement and he found it hard to breathe when he looked at her.

After they moved the cafeteria tables aside so that the car could be pushed into place, Adam handed him the banner and he and Pearl attached it to the car. Then they stood back and Pearl grabbed a hold of his hand. Again.

In huge letters the sign read: "AUCTION OF 1966 SHELBY COBRA! All proceeds to benefit the special education department of the Anderson School

District. Starting bid: $400,000." Underneath that was the website Perk would make live when they got home.

It was beautiful.

Dutch remembered when Adam and Perk had first helped him pick up all his books and papers that Hill had dumped on the ground. He'd thought of them as his best friends then.

Now they really were.

It almost made him want to cry, though he squinted the tears away.

Sometimes, in certain situations, having a facial tic helped.

"What do you guys think?" Adam asked. He stood back with his hands behind his head.

"It's perfect," Dutch said.

CHAPTER 91
Adam

The next order of business was to get the application to Fort Hemsworth Youth Military Boot Camp onto Principal Parmar's desk

The five of them made their way to the main hallway and then into Mr. Parmar's office, where they placed the new application and a pen on his desk.

They all stood around the desk and looked at the application and then at each other. They'd done it.

All the other pranks he and Perk had pulled were thrilling, but nothing compared to this one. This one was actually going to make a difference.

He glanced down at his watch. It wouldn't be a good idea to hang around any longer than necessary.

"All right," he said, "let's get out of here. We'll meet up in the morning and finish it off."

They slapped hands and were exchanging high fives on their way out of Parmar's office when a voice called out in the silence, "Hello? Who's there?"

"Get back in the office," Adam whispered, and pushed Dutch back until they were all hunkered down behind Ms. Gingko's desk—which was difficult, considering how big Ray was.

"Who is it?" Perk whispered.

"I don't know? Mr. Jelepy?"

"What's the janitor doing here at three in the morning?" Perk whispered again.

Adam's heart slammed inside his chest. He had to do something.

He crawled from behind the desk and made his way to the door.

Shoes squeaked down the hallway toward them. Any second the person would turn the corner and they would be trapped in Parmar's office. Adam looked out the door and into the hallway, rifling through his brain for something—anything—that could get them out of this.

His gaze landed on Mr. Berry's room across the hall and slightly to the right. It was as good a plan as any. Adam had to keep whoever it was away from the cafeteria, which was also their escape route, and out of the hallway so they could make a run for it.

He crawled back to the desk. "Take everyone back the way we came," he whispered to Perk. "And be as quiet as you can. Look for me by the parking lot, okay?"

He made to move, but Perk grabbed his arm and held him back. "What are you doing?"

"Don't worry about me," Adam said, grinning. "Just visit me in juvie, okay?"

And he ran.

CHAPTER 92

Perk

Perk's breath caught in his throat when Adam dove into the hallway.

What was he doing?

Two seconds after Adam disappeared, Mr. Jelepy came around the corner, flashlight bobbing.

Perk ducked his head back behind the desk. How was that supposed to help them get away?

Unless he was only saving himself.

"What are we doing? Where's Adam?"

Perk had opened his mouth to answer, even though he didn't know what he was going to say, when the sound of a classroom chair scraping across the floor echoed through the silence.

"Who's there?" Mr. Jelepy called out.

More scraping.

Perk risked crawling to the doorway and looking out into the hallway just as Mr. Jelepy pointed his flashlight into Mr. Berry's room and stepped inside.

More squeaking of desks and chairs across the tile.

He smiled. Adam was risking his neck so they could get away. "Awesome," he whispered. Then he turned to everyone still huddled behind the desk. "Okay, guys, let's go. Hurry!"

Everyone slipped out the door and down the hallway, weaving through the tables in the cafeteria, and then dashed into the gym and out the two double doors. When they were all out, Perk let the doors click shut, never more proud of his best friend. He turned toward everyone bent over their knees, trying to catch their breath in the early morning.

"Where's Adam?" Dutch asked.

"He said to meet him by the windows," Perk said through panted breaths. Which windows again?

"Give me your cell phone," Dutch said.

"What?"

"Just give it to me."

Perk handed it over.

"Pearl, the cell phone numbers," Dutch said. "Did you memorize Mr. Jelepy's?"

"Uh." Pearl looked confused for a moment, then said, "Right" and closed her eyes. Perk watched her eyes flutter under her lids. "Nine-two-one, four-five-two-five."

"You're sure?"

"I think. Mr. Smith asked me to call him when Markus threw up a few months ago."

"What are you going to do?" Perk asked.

Dutch ignored him and dialed the number. "Hello, Jelepy?" Dutch said. "This is Principal Parmar. I know . . . I'm calling from my . . . wife's phone. Uh, I know it seems idiotic to call you at this hour, but I woke up and realized I forgot to tell you something yesterday. Are you at the school tonight? Well, don't go into the cafeteria . . . there's a little surprise that I don't want ruined. Also, it seems like a mouse or gerbil got loose in Mr. Berry's room. I'm having someone come tomorrow." Pause. "Oh, okay. Thank you. See you tomorrow."

Click.

"That was brilliant!" said Perk. He stood up and started around the front of the building. Hopefully Adam was already there. "Come on." They ran, careful to stay in the dark pockets of shadow, until they reached the parking lot.

Perk glanced around. "Adam? Hey, it's us." His stomach twisted. "He said he'd be over here."

"Did he get caught?" Pearl asked. Perk could hear the panic in her voice.

Perk put his hands behind his head, dread filling him. Was Mr. Jelepy the only other person in the school right now? There was a helper that tagged along with Mr. Jelepy sometimes. "No, Adam doesn't get caught. Come on," he whispered, more to himself than anyone. "I don't want to visit you in juvie."

Then there was a rustle of leaves by a nearby window and Adam stood up. "Looks like you won't have to."

CHAPTER 93
Adam

Not many eighth graders arrive early to their middle school in the morning, at least not on purpose. They usually spill out of squeaky bus doors, or dash down the sidewalk with only minutes to spare, hoping to avoid the secretary and her tapping foot and waiting red pen. They slip into chairs just as the bell rings or hand over the late notice. They're never early.

Then again, you only pull a prank like this once in a century.

Adam, Perk, Ray, Dutch, and Pearl were normal, ordinary eighth graders . . . but what is ordinary?

Adam was groggy, having not even gotten back to his room and into his bed until four-thirty, a little more than three hours ago. But thrill still rushed through him.

Everyone looked about as awake as he did, and just as excited.

Perk was already sitting on the curb, his laptop on his lap as he checked the website and made sure it was live. Then he listed Mr. Parmar's Shelby Cobra on as many car auction sites as he could.

"How's it going, Perk?" Adam asked.

He didn't respond but gave them a quick thumbs-up and went back to clicking.

"Dutch, I think it's time to call the paper and TV station using your Hill voice. Make sure they know you're Principal Parmar's proud son. Ray and Pearl, we'll all hang up signs on the doors telling everyone to go straight to the cafeteria. Then all we need is the main attraction."

"Parmar."

CHAPTER 94
Perk

The scene an hour later in the cafeteria was Oscar-worthy—from the set design, to the lead actor, to the paparazzi, to the exciting beginning, all the way to the glory-filled ending.

The crowd gathered in the cafeteria wasn't waiting long before Mr. Parmar rushed in and pushed his way through the sea of clapping students, teachers, and cameramen. Once he reached his car and read the banner, his face turned so white, Perk didn't think any makeup artist would be able to replicate it. "A reporter called me . . . I thought it was a joke. What's the meaning of this? I . . . "

"That was me, Mr. Parmar." A woman stepped

forward with a microphone. "We received a call from your son"—she looked down at her notebook—"Hill Parmar. He let us know about your generous donation for the special education program at the high school. He's so proud of you. Truly, it is such a touching gesture. Please, tell us, what made you do this? What was your motivation?"

"What? I didn't call anyone." Hill's face drained to match his dad's. He looked around at the crowd. "Dad, I didn't call anyone. I promise."

But the woman ignored Hill and shoved the microphone closer to Parmar's face. "Mr. Parmar?"

Parmar's face was like a chameleon, first pale, then splotched with pink, then finally settling on a fierce red. "I . . . I don't know what to say."

"Can you tell us instead how long you had been working on the website to auction off the car and how you managed to keep it hidden from everyone? That is quite a feat."

"Website? Well, I just . . . wanted it to be the best." He held one of the signs they had hung up on the doors in his hand, slowly crumpling it in his fist.

"And, I'm sure you'll be happy to know that since

the website went live this morning, the bidding from people all over the country has already exceeded seven hundred forty thousand."

"I . . . I . . . " He wiped his forehead. "Yes, very surprised." Would he pass out?

"Is there anything else you want to say?"

Mr. Parmar tried to smile, but it looked more like he had to go to the bathroom or he was going to be sick. "I think this gesture," his voice cracked, "umm, speaks for itself."

Perk, for the first time, agreed with him.

It spoke for Tommy and Nish and Dutch and Pearl and Ray and William Bubert and a hundred other kids. Things were gonna change.

CHAPTER 95
Adam

"How about a toast?" Adam said that night.

It was the spring dance, and the five of them stood around the punch bowl just off to the left of Parmar's 1966 Shelby Cobra. The school board thought it would be a good idea to keep it there so that the special education kids who had also, just that day, been invited to the dance, could see the car.

Perk raised his cup of punch to the middle of their group. "To Parmar and Hill," he said.

"Yep. To Parmar and Hill," they all repeated, and took a drink. Adam looked at each of them and then out at the crowd of dancing, chasing, and chitchatting students. "Well," he said. "We did it." He tried to think of something more, but he didn't know what.

Tommy ran up, his cheeks flushed red. "Hi, guys! This is so much fun! Did you see the car?" He pointed to the Shelby Cobra, its paint glinting in the flashing of the disco bulb. "The money goes to us and my school for chairs and windows and computers and stuff."

Perk put his arm around him. "You're right, Tommy. It's all yours."

Adam grinned as his friends congratulated Tommy.

They had all been only yearbook pictures and student files just a month ago.

Now they were 3-D, alive, real. He'd known there was something more, but he never imagined how much more.

He took another swig of punch.

CHAPTER 96
Perk

Tommy dragged Perk onto the dance floor.

Perk had a general rule: no dancing in public . . . ever.

But he let himself join in the ocean of people—
Pearl, Dutch, and Ray surrounding Tommy in a circle
and chanting his name.

He never would've thought that he would trust
these three random people, but he did. He never
thought he'd ever call them friends. But he did.

"Come on, Perk!" Tommy yelled.

Perk grinned and fist-bumped Adam. It was hard to
not move around a little when Tommy was bouncing
and yelling and sweating the way he was, so he made
a little exception.

After all, everyone has exceptions.

CHAPTER 97
Ray

When the slow song came on, Ray bolted for the side where most of the other students were taking refuge behind glasses of punch and pieces of cake. He grabbed a cookie and spotted Mrs. Potter, the school counselor, standing by the lockers watching.

"What are you thinking?" Dutch asked him. "She's a little old for you, don't you think?"

Ray laughed and punched him in the arm. "No, I want to see if maybe I could change some of the classes that I marked down for high school next year. I wasn't really paying attention when we signed up the first time."

"That's cool."

"Yeah," Ray said. "It is."

He glanced at Dutch and grinned. "So are you really going to let her just stand there by the punch bowl?"

"What? Who?" His face reddened when he saw Pearl standing by the half-eaten cake. "Oh."

"Go for it." Ray gently pushed him and then walked over to Mrs. Potter.

"Hi, Mrs. Potter," he said.

"Hello, Ray. Is there something wrong?"

"No, I . . . " His heart clanged against his chest like a loose bolt in an engine. "I had a question about classes next year. I was thinking that I might want to change some of them if it's not too late."

CHAPTER 98
Pearl

Pearl looked up at the clock. Eight-thirty. The dance was almost over.

Then she'd wait outside for her dad and go home. One of her homes. Two homes.

That was normal for her now. Talking and joking and scheming with Dutch, Perk, Ray, and Adam was also normal.

She filled up her cup with punch and watched Adam, Perk, and Tommy bolt off the dance floor and head for the snack table.

"Hey Pearl!" It was Sari.

"Oh, hey, Sari."

Her friend grabbed a cup and guzzled it. "Oh my

gosh, isn't this so much fun? I'm dying of thirst."

"Yeah, it's been a lot of fun." Dutch was talking with Ray. What were they saying?

The song ended.

"All right, middle school students," the DJ said. "This is the last song of the night."

Another slow song started. Was Dutch looking at her? She turned away and smiled as she took a sip from her cup even though there was nothing left.

"Uh, I think that kid," Sari said, "the one that does that weird thing with his face, is trying to get you to come over. Didn't you sit with him at lunch one or two times this week?"

A rush went through Pearl and her fingers pressed imaginary strings.

"Oh my gosh, he's coming over here. Don't worry, I've got your back."

Sari was talking but Pearl wasn't listening.

Someone tapped her shoulder. "Pearl?"

She turned and smiled at Dutch. "Hey."

"Um," Sari said. "Sorry, but she doesn't want to dance."

"What?" Pearl said. "Of course I do. That is . . . if

you want to dance with me."

Sari tugged at her arm. "Come on, Pearl, you don't have to feel sorry for him. I just got a text from my mom and she's outside. You can totally sleep over tonight."

Pearl shrugged her off. "No thanks," she said. "And I don't feel sorry for him."

Dutch squinted and smiled, then held out his hand. She took it and they stepped on to the dance floor.

She didn't want to go back to the before sort of normal. This normal—holding Dutch's hand and hearing Adam, Perk, Ray, and Tommy "oohing" behind them was where she felt more like who she really was.

She could get used to this.

CHAPTER 99

Dutch

Dutch stood outside in the dark and waited for his grandpa.

"Hey, Dutch!"

He turned and saw Adam. "So, me, Ray, and Perk are all going to a movie tomorrow afternoon. Oh, and of course, Pearl." Adam raised his eyebrows up and down. "You want to come?"

Dutch squinted and grinned. "Sure."

"Okay, see you then."

He watched the three of them get into Adam's mom's car and drive off.

"See you, Dutch," Pearl said.

He smiled. Squinted. "See ya."

A car horn honked and he watched her leave.

Thinking back on the day and the dance, it almost seemed impossible. That maybe it had all been a vision.

Gramps pulled up then and Dutch hopped in.

"Did you dance with her?" Gramps asked when he pulled away from the curb.

It was real. "Yep."

Anything was possible.

CHAPTER 100

Adam, Perk, Tommy, Ray, Dutch, and Pearl

Adam, Perk, Tommy, Ray, Dutch, and Pearl all met up at Pearl's dad's apartment the day after school let out.

This was the day they'd been waiting for.

They walked down the sidewalk to the corner of Parmar's street, then cut through a dirt path up the hill above the house. Adam had scoped it out earlier. It was grassy and wide with trees scattered around but open enough. It was the perfect spot for a perfect view.

When they reached the top, they pulled out the blankets and snacks and sat down.

"So when is the bus supposed to come?" Ray asked.

Adam glanced down at his watch. He rubbed his hands together. "Any minute, folks."

"What if Parmar backed out?" Pearl asked.

But the sound of a bus answered her question. They all looked at one another. This was it. When the bus screeched to a halt, a man and a woman in army uniforms stepped off. They looked down at their clipboards and then up at the house.

"This is better than a movie," Dutch said.

"Look! There's Parmar," Perk said.

Mr. Parmar motioned to the front door and then a moment later, Hill slumped up to him, a backpack on his shoulder. He dropped it on the ground and turned to his dad, clearly pleading for him to change his mind.

"It wasn't me that did it. Promise," Dutch said in Hill's voice.

The others laughed.

Mr. Parmar picked up the backpack and slung it over Hill's shoulder again. Then he took the clipboard from the officer and signed a paper.

The two officers saluted and escorted Hill onto the bus.

The door closed. A moment later the bus spit out a cloud of gray smoke and chugged down the road.

"Happy trails, Hill!" Perk said.

Tommy laughed. "Yeah."

Ray knocked Tommy on the arm. "Checkmate, Tommy, right?"

Tommy looked confused for a second then laughed. "Yeah, checkmate! Checkmate."

They all watched the bus disappear. Then they turned and smiled at one another.

It was over.

They'd done it—all of it.

It was over.

"Who wants some snacks?" Adam asked. "I'm starving."

They sat there for a long time. Eventually Adam brought out his lantern and some headlamps. They sat together on the blanket in the grass.

They would be there when the moon came out and they would meet up again in the morning.

Actually, it was just the beginning.

ACKNOWLEDGMENTS

I want to thank my agent, Rebecca Sherman, and my editor, Martha Mihalick, for all the love, support, and care they gave to this book. We've wanted to work together for a good eight years, and now here we are! Martha, I'd do a hundred more revisions under your amazing direction. For the entire team at Greenwillow: copyeditor Anne Dunn; managing editor Tim Smith; cover designer Paul Zakris and illustrators Victoria Jamieson and Mary Kate McDevitt; and Katie Fee, Nellie Kurtzman, and Gina Rizzo in marketing and publicity. I want to give a special thank you to my dearest friend, Kim Nicolas, for not only giving insight into some of the elements of the story but constantly keeping me honest and laughing. To my cousin, Kristin Jiggets, for sharing her and her sisters' experiences growing up—I'm forever grateful and send you huge hugs and crepes—though not cooked inside the belly of a shark. For Monica, who let me sit in her salon while I peppered her with questions about her heritage. To Johanna and her awesome mocha lattes—it was at CuppaJoe where most, if not all, of this book was written and rewritten and revised and then revised again. To my family at SCBWI and all the authors and illustrators in the Rocky Mountains—you make me smile. To my critique group, for just being plain awesome and because I wouldn't be able to write a sentence worth reading without all of you, Thank you always to my beloved family: my mom, dad, Suzanne, and Alisa. I love you so dearly. And to all my nieces and nephews, for asking when my next book is coming out and being little marketers on my behalf: Khloe, Caleb, Sophie, Zach, Sierra, Savannah, Anna, Michael, Daniel, Ryan, Alisa, Judah, Jane, and Caleb. To the furry and scale-y creatures that keep me company at home: Cowboy, Wally, Duchess, Larry, Ulysses, Trixie, and Evie. And last but never least, to the people that make my heart beat: Gracie, Isaac, Ella, Noah, and John-boy. Finally, to God who has done, and continues to do, abundantly more than I've ever thought or imagined. My heart is grateful. My heart is full.